KILLER ON THE LOOSE . . .

"Ah," Clint said, "you're afraid he'll kill another one."

"I'm going to make sure he doesn't kill another woman, or another one of my men."

"Oh," Clint said, "I assume he took your man's gun?"

"No," Stewart said, "he didn't."

"So he's unarmed?"

"He is."

"That ought to make him easier to take."

"I'm not going to take him," Stewart said, "I'm going to kill him."

"That's not very professional, Chief."

"I'm not feeling very professional, Clint," Chief Stewart said. "Not very professional, at all."

J. R. ROBERTS

JOVE BOOKS, NEW YORK

THE LADY KILLERS

A Jove Book / published by arrangement with
the author

PRINTING HISTORY
Jove edition / July 1998

The Penguin Putnam Inc. World Wide Web site address is
http://www.penguinputnam.com

ISBN: 0-515-12303-X

A JOVE BOOK®
Jove Books are published by The Berkley Publishing Group,
a member of Penguin Putnam Inc.,
200 Madison Avenue, New York, New York 10016.
JOVE and the "J" design are trademarks belonging to Jove
Publications, Inc.

PRINTED IN THE UNITED STATES OF AMERICA

10 9 8 7 6 5 4 3 2 1

THE
GUNSMITH
198
THE LADY KILLERS

ONE

Clint couldn't see the Island House from the ferry, but he could see Fort Mackinac very clearly. The fort was in perfect position to defend the Straits of Mackinac, which separated the lower peninsula of Michigan from the upper, and also joined Lake Huron and Lake Michigan.

It had been several years since he had met Capt. Henry Van Allen. Capt. Van Allen had been a skipper on the Great Lakes for many years, and several years ago he had gone west to see the Mississippi, and meet some of its riverboat captains. On one of the riverboats he and Clint had met, and Van Allen told Clint that he was retired many years from piloting the Great Lakes and was operating a hotel on Mackinac Island. He had invited Clint to come to see the hotel and the island. Now, three years later, Clint was hoping that the invitation was still open. He had sent a telegram ahead, announcing his intention to visit, but had not been in any one place long enough since then to have received a response, be it positive or negative.

Clint had made his way from Texas to Michigan on horseback and by rail and had finally ridden into Mackinac City, which was right across from Mackinac Island. The island was as Van Allen had described it, serene and beautiful. One of the more beautiful sights was the Grand Hotel, which was off to the left of the fort, and the town.

Before Clint disembarked from the ferry, one of the crew

told him to be sure to see something called Arch Rock. Clint said he would, but didn't ask where or what it was. He was sure Van Allen would tell him.

The Island House, owned by Henry Van Allen since 1865, was in the shadow of the fort, east of the business section of the small French town. Except for the town, and the section where the Grand Hotel stood, the island was largely uninhabited and undeveloped.

Clint found the Island House with no trouble, but noticed another building nearby called Mackinac Sanitarium. He understood that the island was a place used not only for vacations, but also for convalescence.

He walked Duke up to the front entrance, but before he could mount the steps the front door opened and Capt. Henry Van Allen came rushing out. He was as Clint remembered, tall, gray-haired, bearded, standing ramrod straight despite his advanced years, and looking every inch the Great Lakes skipper he had been for many years.

"My good friend!" he exclaimed, running down the steps like a man half his age.

"Captain—"

Van Allen reached Clint and, ignoring the proffered hand, captured the younger man in a crushing hug. Only then did he stand back and accept the hand.

"How good of you to come," Van Allen said, pumping Clint's hand enthusiastically.

"I wasn't sure the invitation was still open," Clint said. "After all, it's been several years."

"Ah! What are a few years to a man my age?" Van Allen demanded. "Come, let's get your horse looked after so you can come inside and have a look."

A man named Simon appeared, and Van Allen explained how Simon had been with him for many years when he was the captain of his own ship. Now the man cared for the livery stable, as well as many other duties.

"For which," Simon commented good-naturedly, "I am grossly underpaid."

"Can you handle him, Simon?" Clint asked. "He's not the friendliest of animals."

"He's a big one, too," Simon said, "but I'll handle him, sir."

It was hard to gauge Simon's age. He was younger than Van Allen, and since the captain had been retired from the Lakes for almost twenty years, Simon must have started with Van Allen when he was very young.

"All right, now," Van Allen said. "The grand tour. It's not the Grand Hotel, but I think you'll like it. This way, this way."

Van Allen led the way up the steps, and Clint had to trot to keep up with him.

TWO

During the ferry ride out, the Grand Hotel—"Plank's Grand Hotel," the crewman had said—had been pointed out to Clint. Even at a distance the place was very impressive. Van Allen's Island House was certainly not equal to the Grand, but it was impressive to Clint nevertheless.

Downstairs was a large dining room and sitting room, with big windows in the front to afford a view of the street. There was also a porch in front that wrapped around the side of the building. During the day, Van Allen said, many of the guests would sit out there, drink beverages, play cards games, or simply relax.

"Of course," Van Allen continued, "this being late September the season is just about over and we don't have as many guests as we did during the summer."

"How many rooms do you have, Henry?" Clint asked.

"A dozen."

"And how many are occupied now?"

"Presently," Van Allen said, "there are four, but several of those guests will be checking out by the end of the month."

"I see."

"Come," Van Allen said, "see the kitchen, and then I will show you my den."

Clint followed Van Allen through the dining room and into the kitchen.

• • •

Upstairs, in Room Three, an argument was in progress. It was not a new argument, but one which had been raging for several weeks—and perhaps longer. After all, the principals were a married couple, and even married couples cannot always tell how long they have been arguing about the same subject.

Gerald McCrain was a businessman and the month he and his wife had spent on the island, in Henry Van Allen's inn, had been his first vacation in over twelve years. Fifty-three years of age, he had started working for a living when he was fourteen and was a self-made man. He owned several steel mills in Pittsburgh, and was of the opinion that every one of them had either fallen down or gone out of business while he had been gone.

Jessica McCrain had been married to Gerald for eight years. Now thirty-two, more than twenty years his junior, she had married him when he was already a wealthy man. During the eight years they had been together he had more than doubled that wealth.

"I don't want to leave three days early," Jessica snapped at Gerald.

"We've been here four weeks, Jess," McCrain argued, "what will leaving three days early hurt? Besides, you've been miserable the whole time."

Not the whole time, she thought, remembering her dalliance with a young carriage driver not long after they had arrived. At least he had shown the proper respect to her well-rounded, smooth-skinned body. McCrain would have paid her more attention if she covered her naked body with steel soot.

"You are the one who has made me miserable, Gerald," she said, "with your constant worry about your precious mills."

"It's those mills, dear lady, that clothe you and buy you your jewelry, if I may be so bold as to remind you."

"You are always reminding me of that, Gerald," she retorted, "every chance you get."

McCrain turned to look out the window. He was dressed, even on vacation, in a business suit. It was his way of protesting having been dragged away from Pittsburgh to this godforsaken island. When he turned back he regarded his wife. Clad in a simple sundress, she was sitting in the room's easy chair. She was a well-built woman, robust some might say, tall and solid and very beautiful, and she sat in the chair as if it would take dynamite to pry her out of it. Her long blond hair was hanging softly past her shoulders, partially obscuring the spray of freckles on her chest, just above the V of her cleavage. Those freckles had been the first thing to attract McCrain's eyes nine years ago, when they'd first met. Now he hardly noticed them.

"Jessica—"

"You can leave if you want to, Gerald," she said, cutting him off. "I am not."

How had he failed to notice what a shrew she was—or was she, eight years ago when they had first married? Probably not. Or if she was, she had hidden it until after the wedding, until after getting rid of her would cost him dearly if he tried.

"Jessica," McCrain said, "I'm growing tired of your . . . your obstinacy."

"Obstinacy? Is that what you call not wanting to have my vacation ruined? Obstinate? Well, let me tell you, Gerald McCrain . . ."

In Room Five, down the hall, Mary Morgan looked at her mother, Julia, and said, "They're at it again."

"I can hear," said Julia Morgan from her chair. She did not look up from her knitting.

"Mother," Mary said, "let's go for a walk."

"That's all you ever want to do, Mary," Julia said, "is walk. You have young legs, you know, while mine are old and feeble."

Mary Morgan was twenty-five and her mother was not yet fifty. She was anything but feeble, but she did hate walking. The island was so beautiful, however, that Mary wanted to see every inch of it—and she did not want to sit in their room and listen to the McCrains argue.

"You go on," Julia said. "I'll just stay here and relax."

"Mother—"

"I'll tell you what the outcome of the argument is."

"We know what the outcome will be," Mary said, throwing a wrap over her shoulders. "That poor man is the most henpecked—"

Now Julia looked up.

"Poor man? All that poor woman wants is a vacation, and that cad is trying to cut it short."

Mary adjusted her auburn hair so it lay over the wrap and not beneath it.

"You'd do well, young lady, to find yourself an older, successful man and then henpeck him the way Mrs. McCrain does hers. She knows how to keep a man in line."

Mary knew for a fact that Julia had henpecked her father to death and also called it "keeping him in line." She wanted to get out of the room before her mother started telling stories about her father again.

"Why, your father, God rest his soul—"

"I'm going to go for a walk, Mother," Mary said, hurrying to the door.

"Well, be back for dinner, dear."

"I will," Mary said. "Bye."

And she fled the room, followed all the way down the hall by the angry tones of Mr. and Mrs. Gerald McCrain.

THREE

Van Allen introduced Clint to the cook, Mrs. Livingstone, and asked if he was hungry and would like a snack before dinner.

"No snack before dinner," Mrs. Livingstone said. "We'll be eating in one hour."

"There you have it," Van Allen said helplessly. "She is the mistress of the kitchen, Clint. Can you wait an hour?"

"If it's going to taste as good as it smells I can," Clint said.

"I don't think you'll be disappointed," Mrs. Livingstone, a portly woman in her early fifties, promised him.

"I can believe it, Mrs. Livingstone," Clint said. "From the looks and smells of this kitchen, you must not only be mistress of the kitchen, but a master cook, as well."

"I like this one," Mrs. Livingstone said to Van Allen. "He's not like the other male guests." She looked quickly at Clint. "You are a guest, aren't you?"

"I am."

"Not a paying guest," Van Allen hurried to point out. "My guest."

"A guest is a guest to me," she said, "but something tells me, Mr. Adams, that you are different."

Clint gallantly took Mrs. Livingstone's hand, kissed it, and said, "If only you would let me show you."

"Get this one out of here, Captain," she said, "before I decide to keep him."

"Out, Clint," Van Allen said, "out of the kitchen. I don't know what you've done, but the woman likes you. You'll have to watch out for her now. She might drag you to her room."

"No 'might' about it," the woman said. "First chance I get."

"I might never want to leave," Clint said as Van Allen pushed him out of the room.

"What are you doing, man?" Van Allen demanded. "Don't flirt with my cook."

"She seems like a nice woman."

"She hates men," Van Allen said, then added, "except, apparently, for you."

"I'll be on the lookout," Clint said. "If dinner's in an hour I'll need to clean up."

"I'll show you to your room," Van Allen said. "I'm a poor host. You probably would like to rest, and here I'm giving you the tour already. Come with me."

They walked back to the entry foyer just in time to see a pretty young woman come down the stairs.

"Oh!" she said, putting her hand to her bosom. "You startled me, Captain."

"Please forgive me, Miss Morgan," Van Allen said, "and allow me to present a friend of mine who has only just arrived. Clint Adams, this lovely young lady is Miss Mary Morgan. Miss Morgan, my friend Clint Adams."

"Mr. Adams," she said, looking Clint up and down with interest, "a pleasure."

"Miss Morgan," Clint said, "the pleasure is mine. Are you . . . staying here alone?"

"Oh, heavens, no," she said, "I am here with my mother. We are from Boston."

"I've been to Boston," Clint said. "Lovely city—although probably less so since you are here, and not there."

"Mr. Adams," Mary Morgan said, "I can see you are a

Westerner. I've heard how charming the men of the West are. You seem to be proving the point."

"Where are you off to, Miss Morgan?" Van Allen asked before Clint could reply.

"Just for a walk around the island, Captain."

"Well, dinner is in an hour, and you know how Mrs. Livingstone gets when guests are late for dinner."

"Now you sound like my mother, Captain," Mary said. "Rest assured I shall return in time for dinner. Will you be joining us, Mr. Adams?"

"Indeed I will, Miss Morgan."

"I'll look forward to it, then," she said, and went out the front door.

"That's two," Van Allen said.

"Two what?"

"Two women you've charmed and you've been here less than a half an hour."

"It's a curse," Clint said.

At that moment they heard a door slam upstairs and then another woman appeared at the top of the stairs. While Mary Morgan had been pretty and young, this woman was stunning, probably in her thirties. She was blond, and her hair hung to her shoulders. Although he was not at the best vantage point to tell, she seemed to Clint to be showing an interesting expanse of cleavage. He'd know better when she came down the stairs.

"Uh-oh," Van Allen said.

"Who is that?" Clint asked.

"That," Van Allen said, "is Mrs. Gerald McCrain. Don't try to charm her, Clint. Her husband is very rich and powerful in Pittsburgh."

"But we're not in Pittsburgh, Henry," Clint said as the woman started down the stairs, "are we?"

FOUR

Both men waited and watched as the woman seemed to glide down the stairs.

"Captain Van Allen," she said as she reached the bottom, "how nice to see you."

"Mrs. McCrain."

Clint's eyes were drawn to the spray of freckles across the top of her cleavage. Freckles like that—usually seen on redheads, not blondes—often made him imagine licking them.

"And who's this stranger?" she asked.

"My name is Clint Adams," he said, "and it's my pleasure to meet you, Mrs. McCrain."

"Mr. Adams," she said, extending her hand, "how nice to have an interesting-looking man in the inn." And then with a glance at Van Allen she added, "Excuse me, two interesting-looking men."

"Is your husband not here with you, then?" Clint asked hopefully.

"Oh, he is here," she said. "He's upstairs in our room, and he is not so interesting-looking as you are, Mr. Adams. I'm afraid, in fact, that we have just had a terrible fight, and I don't find him particularly interesting at all, at the moment."

"I'm sorry to hear that."

"Were you, uh, going out, ma'am?" Van Allen asked.

"Just for a short walk."

"You just missed Mary Morgan," Clint said, "who has also gone for a walk."

"Such a sweet child, don't you think?" Jessica McCrain asked.

"She seemed very nice," Clint said.

"Perhaps I can catch up to her and we can walk together."

"I'll give you the same warning I gave her, Mrs. McCrain," Van Allen said. "Mrs. Livingstone is putting dinner on the table in an hour—less than an hour now."

"Oh," Jessica McCrain said, "I'm sure we'll be back in plenty of time—unless we get involved in girl talk." She looked pointedly at Clint. "Now that we have something to talk about."

"It was a pleasure to meet you, Mrs. McCrain," Clint said sincerely. "I look forward to dinner, and to meeting your husband."

"Please," she said, "call me Jessica. It will make my husband furious."

"As you wish," Clint said.

"Gentlemen," she said, and went out the door. Clint doubted that this woman and Mary Morgan would have very much in common at all.

"That is a lot of woman," Clint said.

"I'm warning you—"

"I know," Clint said, "her husband is very rich and powerful—in Cleveland."

"Pittsburgh."

"Wherever."

"Well," Van Allen said, "thank God there are no more women here for you to charm. Come with me and I'll show you to your room—which, by the way, is very far from the Morgan and McCrain rooms."

"Pity," Clint said, and followed Van Allen up the stairs.

• • •

The room was small but well furnished and very comfortable. On the bed were Clint's saddlebags, no doubt left there by Simon.

"We all dine together," Van Allen told Clint. "This is more an inn than a hotel."

"I'll be down in time," Clint assured him.

"Water basin and pitcher on the dresser," Van Allen said. "Towels are in the dresser. If you need anything else, just let me know."

"Do you have any more staff other than Mrs. Livingstone and Simon?" Clint asked.

"Oh, shit," Van Allen said.

"What is it?"

"I forgot about Patricia," the older man said. "You'll probably charm her, as well."

"Who is Patricia?"

"She's the maid," Van Allen said. "She'll see to your needs—and I mean your linen needs, and such."

"I know what you meant, Henry."

"She's Mary Morgan's age and very impressionable," Van Allen said. "You'll turn her head with two words, I'll warrant."

"Don't worry, Henry," he said. "I'll be surly to the girl."

"Don't do that, for pity's sake," Van Allen said, "you'll scare her away. Just don't be so damned—oh, what's the use. You probably can't help yourself. I'll see you at dinner."

"I'll be there."

Van Allen left, and Clint laughed and shook his head. Already his stay promised to be an interesting one. He was glad he had come.

FIVE

Clint cleaned up, put on fresh clothes, and made sure he was in the dining room in plenty of time for dinner. Because he was on an island far from the western towns he was used to, he left his gun belt in his room. He did, however, tuck his little Colt New Line into the back of his belt and donned a jacket to cover it. The jacket was the only one he had with him, buckskin with fringe.

As he entered the dining room he saw Jessica McCrain standing off to one side with a man easily twenty years her senior. The man was frowning. She smiled when she saw Clint and hurried to greet him, which made her husband frown even more.

"Clint," she said, "how nice to see you."

She was obviously trying to rile her husband, since they had just seen each other half an hour ago.

"Hello, Jessica," he said, taking her proferred hand. She held his hand much longer than was necessary.

"I'd like you to meet my husband," she said. Judging by the hot looks she was giving him, Clint thought she would probably rather be dragging him upstairs to one of the bedrooms than introducing him to her husband.

"Clint Adams," she said, pulling him across the room, "this is my husband, Gerald McCrain."

"Mr. McCrain," Clint said, "it's nice to meet you."

The two men shook hands and sized one another up.

"Your name is familiar to me, Adams," McCrain said. Clint disliked people who immediately dropped the "Mister" from in front of his name. It was something someone did when he felt superior to you.

"Really?" Clint asked. "I never heard your name before today."

"Then you're not from the East," McCrain said. "Everybody in the East has heard of McCrain Steel."

"Darling," Jessica McCrain said, "you can tell by looking at Mr. Adams that he's not from the East. He has that . . . rugged Western look."

"You call it rugged," McCrain said, "I call it . . . uncivilized. Let's get to the table."

McCrain moved away from his wife and walked toward the table.

"I'm sorry," she said. "He's rude."

"You don't have to apologize for him."

"Oh, yes," she said, "I do, constantly." Then she followed her husband to the dinner table.

Clint turned just in time to see Mary Morgan enter the dining room with another woman, probably her mother. However, the older woman seemed to only be in her late forties, and she was quite handsome. It was easy to see where the daughter got her looks from.

"Miss Morgan," Clint asked, "how was your walk?"

"It was quite pleasant, thank you," Mary Morgan said. "Mr. Adams, I'd like you to meet my mother, Mrs. Julia Morgan."

"A pleasure," Clint said, looking at Julia. "It's not difficult to see where your daughter gets her beauty from, Mrs. Morgan."

"My daughter warned me you were charming, Mr. Adams," Julia Morgan said. "She neglected to tell me, however, that you were a rascal."

"Mother!"

"That's a harsh judgment to make on first meeting, Mrs. Morgan."

"Nonsense, Mr. Adams," Julia said, "I happen to like rascals. I was married to one for a very long time."

With that she continued on to the dinner table, greeting the others who were seated there.

"My father," Mary Morgan said, "was a rascal."

"Was?"

"He died several years ago."

"Then your mother is a widow."

"Yes."

"Any rascals in her life at the present time?"

"None, I fear," Mary said.

"Why do you fear?"

"She's taken up knitting."

"And that's a bad thing?"

Mary Morgan laughed.

"My mother is too young to sit and knit, Mr. Adams," she said. "Perhaps you noticed that?"

"As a matter of fact, Miss Morgan," he said, "I did."

"I was hoping you would," she said, "and you can call me Mary."

Clint frowned and said, "You wouldn't be planning a little matchmaking, would you, Mary?"

"Only of the most harmless kind, Mr. Adams."

"Clint."

She smiled and said, "Clint," then followed her mother to the table.

"Still at it, I see," Henry Van Allen said, coming up behind Clint.

"At what?" Clint asked innocently.

"Working on the mother now?" Van Allen asked. "The daughter isn't enough for you?"

"I've only just met the woman," Clint said, looking over to where Mary Morgan was seating herself next to her mother, "and already she's branded me a rascal."

"Oh?" Van Allen said. "And is that the first time you've worn that brand?"

"On such short acquaintance, Henry," Clint said, "yes."

SIX

During dinner Clint sat just to Captain Henry Van Allen's left; the former Great Lakes skipper sat at the head of the table. Across from Clint, to the captain's right, was Gerald McCrain. To Clint's left was Mary Morgan.

The dinner had not only been prepared by Mrs. Livingstone, but served as wcll. It was a wonderfully tasty chicken, with full complement of vegetables, and when she served Clint he noticed that he got just a little more than the others did.

"There's that charm at work again," said Van Allen, who also noticed the extra large portions.

Clint changed the subject.

"I thought you said four of your rooms were occupied," he said. "Where are the other two guests?"

"They're both gentlemen," Van Allen said, "who are a bit . . . odd."

"In what way?"

"Well, one of them says he's a scientist of some sort who came here to do experiments."

"What's odd about that?"

"He goes out early in the morning," Van Allen said, "and returns at night. He never seems to take anything with him. Doesn't a scientist need instruments of some kind?"

"I would think so."

"Well, then, where are his?"

"Maybe they're in his room?"

"Not that I saw when he checked in," Van Allen said, "and the maid hasn't seen anything, either."

"And what about the other man?"

"Him," Van Allen said. "He never comes out of his room. He asked if he could have his meals served to him there."

"And you agreed?"

Van Allen shrugged and said, "He's paying extra for the privilege."

"Mr. Adams."

Clint looked across the table. Jessica McCrain was sitting to her husband's right, smiling across at him.

"Yes, Mrs. McCrain?"

"I thought we agreed you'd call me Jesse?"

"Uh, all right, Jesse."

"Tell us, how long do you intend to stay here on Mackinac?"

"I'm not sure, Mrs.—Jesse," Clint said. "I've only just arrived."

"Mr. Adams is a friend of mine come to visit," Van Allen said. "We have some catching up to do."

"I imagine you'll want to show him the island," Jesse said.

"Well, yes, indeed."

"Don't forget to show him Arch Rock."

"One of the crewmen on the ferry mentioned that."

"It's a natural rock formation that's quite beautiful," Mary Morgan said.

Clint looked at Mary and said, "I'll have to make sure I see it." He looked past her to her mother. "Have you seen it, Mrs. Morgan?"

"I can't say that I have, Mr. Adams."

"Why not?"

She smiled—hardly a smile at all, just a brief movement of her lips—and said, "I have other things to do, I'm afraid."

Clint decided to let the matter drop.

"I haven't seen it myself," Jesse said, reclaiming Clint's attention. "Perhaps we could see it together?"

Clint saw Gerald McCrain start, look at his wife, and then across the table at him.

"Well, Jesse, I imagine your husband would like to see it with you—"

"Damned foolishness, looking at some rock!" Gerald McCrain announced. "She can look at it with you, if she wants."

"There, see?" Jesse said. "He doesn't mind. Shall we say tomorrow morning, bright and early?"

"Well . . . I suppose so," Clint said, not sure what was going on. "After breakfast?"

"That will be wonderful," Jesse said. She looked across the table at the two Morgan women, mother and daughter, with an odd expression of triumph on her face, as if there'd been some competition going on.

If there had been, Clint was entirely in the dark about it.

After dinner Gerald and Jesse McCrain went back to their room, as did Julia Morgan. Mary announced she was going to sit out on the porch. Henry Van Allen invited Clint into his study for a glass of port.

When they were both seated with a glass Van Allen said, "Do you know what you're doing?"

"About what?"

"Going to see Arch Rock with Jessica McCrain."

"You saw what happened," Clint said. "I had to be polite. Besides, her husband practically insisted."

"That's a dangerous man, Clint."

"So you've told me," Clint said. "I don't intend to do anything, Henry."

"It ain't *your* intentions I'm worried about, lad," Van Allen said.

SEVEN

While they were sitting in the study there was a knock at the door and Simon entered.

"Captain," he said, "Chief Stewart is here to see you."

"Show him in, Simon," Van Allen said.

"An ex-mate?" Clint asked.

Van Allen shook his head.

"Chief Anson Stewart is the chief of police here on Mackinac," Van Allen said.

"What brings him here?"

"We're friends," Van Allen said, "and he likes my port. Also, we've been having some problems on the island, of late."

"What kind of problems?"

"Perhaps that's why he's here," Van Allen said. "I'll let him tell you."

Simon reappeared with a barrel-chested man in tow. The man had an overcoat on, as it got chilly on the island in the evenings. Beneath the coat he seemed to be wearing blue pants, which may or may not have been part of a uniform. He was red-faced, which could have been from the lake air, but Clint had an idea it was from something else.

"Anson," Van Allen said, standing up. "What brings you here?"

"Just came for a talk, Henry," the chief said. "I didn't know I'd be interrupting anything."

"You're not," Van Allen said. "I'd like you to meet a friend of mine. Anson Stewart, this is Clint Adams."

Clint rose and shook hands with the man, who had a firm grip.

"From the West?"

"Yes."

"Henry's told me about you, Mr. Adams."

"Don't believe everything Henry says, Chief Stewart," Clint said.

"I'm a policeman, Mr. Adams," Stewart said. "I automatically believe only half of what anyone tells me—and with Henry, it's less than that."

"Would you like a glass of port while you're casting aspersions on me, Anson?"

"I would love one."

While Van Allen poured, the chief of police unbuttoned his coat and removed it. He was, indeed, wearing a uniform jacket beneath it. There was a third chair in the room and he took it. Van Allen handed him a glass of port and sat in his own chair again.

"I was starting to tell Clint that we've been having some trouble on the island of late," Van Allen said. "I thought perhaps you'd like to finish."

"It's not such a little problem," Chief Stewart said. He looked at Van Allen, then back at Clint. "We've had two girls murdered on the island."

"Murdered? How?"

"Stabbed."

"Raped?"

"No."

"Young girls?"

"Young women, I should say."

"When did this happen?"

"First one happened three weeks ago," Stewart said, "the second one just last week."

"Any suspects?"

The chief, who sported a well-cared-for mustache, tugged at the end of it and said, "A whole island full of them."

"Do you have someone working on it?" Clint asked.

"Whataya mean?"

"I mean a detective."

"Detective?" Stewart said. "I've got a four-man police department, Mr. Adams, and I make five. The closest thing to a detective I have . . . well, I don't have *anything* close to a detective."

"What about some federal help?" Clint asked. "You could send for a marshal."

"I did that already, right after the second girl was killed."

"And?"

"They said someone would be here as soon as possible. Meanwhile, I'm it."

"And if a marshal doesn't get here soon," Van Allen said, "the people on this island will scatter to the four winds. It gets pretty deserted on this island in the winter."

"In fact," Stewart said, "the killer could be gone even now."

"Well, that wouldn't be so bad, would it?"

"That depends."

"On what?"

"On if he comes back again."

"Again?" Clint looked at Van Allen.

"We had the same thing last year," he said.

"And the year before," the chief added.

"Three years in a row?"

The chief and Van Allen exchanged a glance, and then Stewart looked at Clint and said, "Five."

"Whoa," Clint said, moving forward in his chair. "You have a killer who's come to the island five years in a row?"

"Comes here, or lives here," Stewart said. "He kills three girls, and then stops."

"And the government hasn't put a marshal here to look into it?"

"They have," Stewart said, "every year, and he finds nothing. I think that's why they're so slow to send someone this year."

"They're waiting for the third one so they won't have to," Clint said.

Stewart nodded. "That's what I think."

"That's crazy."

"Why?" Stewart asked. "It's controlled, it's limited to the island and none of the surrounding areas. What do they care?"

"But . . . five years?"

Stewart stared into his glass of port.

"I was hoping to put a stop to it this year," he said, "but I haven't got much time. Once he takes his third victim, he'll stop."

Clint was amazed that he had chosen this precise time to come to the island. He'd thought that by coming here and spending a little time he'd be able to get away from other people's problems.

"Less and less people have been coming to the island each year," Van Allen told him. "That's why I only have four rooms rented out."

"What about the sanitarium next door?" Clint asked.

"They claim nobody can get out," Stewart said. "It's still my best bet, though. I've had a man watching it for the past week."

"Are they losing business, as well?" Clint asked. It was what he'd meant in the first place.

"Everybody is," Stewart said. "I'm surprised they haven't fired me by now."

"That wouldn't be fair," Van Allen said. "It's only the summer—August and September, actually—that this happens."

"By the time he takes his next victim," Stewart said,

"that will be fifteen dead girls. That sounds like a good enough reason to fire me, doesn't it?"

Clint had to admit that it did.

"Well, if they do fire you maybe we can leave the island together," Van Allen said.

"You're going to leave?" Clint asked.

"I can't last another season with mostly empty rooms, Clint," Van Allen said. "I'll have to do something."

"You love this place, Henry," Chief Stewart said.

"Yes, I do," Van Allen admitted, "and to tell you the truth, I might not even be able to find a buyer. I might have to sell it real cheap."

Stewart and Van Allen sipped their port and pondered the changes that might be coming into their lives.

"Maybe we can stop him," Clint said.

"We?" Stewart asked.

"If you'll accept my help."

"I'll take all the help I can get, Mr. Adams."

"That would be great," Van Allen said. "Clint's real good at this kind of thing, Anson. He was a lawman once."

"What would you suggest we do, Mr. Adams?" Stewart asked.

"I'm not sure right now, Chief," Clint said. "Let me think about it overnight—but I think, from this point on, you should start calling me Clint."

"All right, Clint."

"Well," Van Allen said, "I think this calls for another glass of port."

Clint agreed and held out his glass, hoping he hadn't just made a mistake.

EIGHT

Clint left Chief Stewart and Captain Van Allen in the study and went out onto the porch. He'd forgotten that Mary Morgan had gone out there, and apparently startled her as he came out.

"I'm sorry," he said. "I didn't mean to scare you."

"You didn't scare me," she said, "you just surprised me."

"I just thought I'd come out for some air," he said. "It's pretty out here."

"Yes, it is," she said, "but I was about to go in. It's chilly."

She rubbed her hands up and down her bare arms.

"Here," he said, taking off his jacket, "this will keep you warm and you can stay a little longer."

She accepted the jacket as he draped it over her shoulders.

"Thank you," she said. "You're very kind."

"Your mother seems to think I'm a rascal, though."

"She thinks all men are rascals," Mary said, "especially the smooth-talking ones."

"Like me?"

She nodded.

"You and my dad."

"He was a smooth talker?"

"Mother says he could talk the bark off a tree. I never saw that side of him."

"Did he die when you were young?"

"No," she said, "he died two years ago, as a matter of fact . . . I just never saw that side of him. I . . . remember him differently."

"You don't have to talk about this if it upsets you," he said.

"It doesn't upset me anymore," she said. "My father may have been this dashing, charming figure to my mother, but he was always mean and harsh with me."

"Couldn't it be that your childhood memories—"

"It wasn't just during my childhood," she said. "It was when I got older. In fact, the closer I got to being a woman, the meaner he got."

"I'm sorry to ask, but did he—I mean—"

"No," she said, "nothing like that. He was just . . . a mean, cruel man, that's all."

"But your mother doesn't remember him that way?"

"Of course not," Mary said. "She remembers the dashing young man she married. I guess I can't really blame her for wanting to remember him that way."

"I get the impression your mother doesn't come out of her room very much."

"Really only for meals," Mary said. "This vacation was my idea, and I had to drag her. She doesn't let me forget it."

"Have you been walking the island alone much, Mary?" he asked. He suddenly remembered that she had taken a walk that evening alone. Jesse McCrain had also left the inn alone, but Mary Morgan was the one who fit the description of the two dead girls more than the older woman.

"Are you thinking about those girls who were killed?" she asked.

Clint was glad she had brought it up. He wasn't sure if the guests knew about the murders.

"Yes, that was what I was thinking about."

"I'm not frightened."

"Why not?"

"I don't think he'd pick me."

"Why not?"

"From what I've heard," she said, "he seems to be preying on pretty young women."

"And you don't think you match that description?"

"I'm rather plain."

Clint was amazed that the woman didn't know how pretty she was.

"Is that what your father used to tell you?" hc asked. "That you were plain?"

She hesitated, then said, "Among other things."

"Mary, you're very—"

Abruptly she swung his jacket off her shoulders and held it out to him.

"I should be going in."

He accepted the jacket, but as she turned to leave he grabbed her arm.

"Promise me you won't go walking alone anymore."

"It doesn't matter," she said. "We'll be leaving soon."

"Promise me."

She stared at him, then relented.

"All right, I promise."

"Good night, then."

"Good night."

She went inside, leaving him alone on the porch. The island was quiet, and the sky was filled with stars. Next door he could only see a few lights from the sanitarium. He wondered if there was a killer inside there or if it was someone else, somebody more respectful on the island. A local merchant, perhaps. Then again it could have been a returning guest, someone who came every year at the same time. He wondered if the police chief had questioned Van Allen's two strange male guests yet.

That would be his first suggestion to Chief Stewart in the morning.

NINE

Clint was still on the porch when Chief Stewart came out.

"I've got to head home," he said when he saw Clint. "I've got a wife who worries."

"Mind if I ask you a question?" Clint asked.

"Go ahead."

"Have you questioned the two men who are staying here?"

"I talked to the man who doesn't leave his room."

"Did you see him?"

Stewart shook his head.

"It's very odd," he said. "He wouldn't open the door and let me in, but he talked to me through the door."

"That is odd," Clint said. "Do you think he's afraid you'll recognize him?"

"I hadn't thought of that," Stewart said. "You think he might be some well-known outlaw hiding out on our island?"

"I don't know. What did you think?"

"I thought he had some sort of skin disease," Stewart said. "You know, the kind that would keep him from coming out in the sun? I thought perhaps he didn't want anyone to see him."

"I guess that's a possibility. What about the other man, the one who says he's a scientist?"

"I haven't talked to him yet," Stewart said. "It seems as if he's never here when I come."

"Has either man stayed here before?" Clint asked. "Maybe when the other murders were committed?"

Stewart looked chagrined.

"I told you I wasn't a detective," he said. "I haven't asked that."

"I'll check with Henry, see if they've stayed here before."

"There are other hotels on the island," Stewart said. "I'll check with them, too."

"We can compare notes," Clint said.

Stewart stuck out his hand.

"I appreciate your offer of help, Clint. Maybe together we can put a stop to this."

Clint shook the man's hand and said, "I hope so, Chief."

As the chief went down the steps and walked off into the night, Henry Van Allen came out onto the porch.

"I've told Anson all about you, Clint," he said. "He's real excited that you're here to help."

"What exactly did you tell him, Henry?"

"I told him that you were much more than just your reputation with a gun," Van Allen explained. "I said you'd been through this kind of thing a time or two before, caught yourself one or two murderers in the past."

Clint couldn't fault Van Allen for anything he'd said. It was all true.

"I'm no detective, either, Henry," he said.

"More of one than poor Anson, though, I'll warrant."

"Well," Clint said reluctantly, "maybe so. Tell me, Henry. These two men who are staying here, what are their names?"

"The scientist fella, his name is—let's see, what is it?"

"Why don't we go inside and take a look at your records? We can get their names and find out if they've ever been here before."

"That's a fine idea, Clint," Van Allen said, "a fine idea—and we can have another glass of port while we're at it."

TEN

There was a knock on Clint's door later that night, after everyone had gone to sleep. He wasn't asleep yet, though. He was lying on his back with his hands clasped behind his head, contemplating what he had gotten himself into this time. Finding a killer of fourteen women on an island he wasn't familiar with would not be easy. He was going to have to work closely with the chief of police, which meant getting to know the man better.

At the sound of the knock he got off the bed and walked barefoot to the door. He was shirtless but still wearing his jeans. When he opened the door and saw Jessica McCrain standing there in a robe, he wasn't surprised.

"You're not surprised," she said with a smile. "Good."

"Jesse, this isn't a good idea."

"Let me in."

"No."

"If you don't," she said, "I'll start screaming."

"You'll wake the whole house."

"That's the idea."

He sighed and backed away to let her in. As she passed him he caught the scent of her perfume, and of something else. Despite himself, he was reacting.

He closed the door and turned to face her.

"What do you want, Jesse?"

"You know what I want. You've been looking at me all day."

"You've been looking at me," he countered.

"Well," she said, "you wouldn't know that if you hadn't been looking at me, would you?"

She had a point there.

She moved closer to him then and he stood his ground.

"What would your husband say if he caught you here, Jesse?"

"He's not going to catch me," she said. "Besides, I don't think he'd care all that much."

"But I don't—"

She cut him off with a kiss. The minute her lips touched his, she pressed her hand to his crotch, feeling him hard there. Her lips were sweet, there was no denying that, and as her tongue pushed into his mouth he put his arms around her and pulled her to him. Her breasts were big and solid against his chest.

"I can't wait—" she gasped, wrenching her lips from his.

She backed away from him and pulled the string that held her robe together at the neck. She dropped the robe to the ground, revealing a flimsy nightgown beneath it. That, too, dropped to the floor and then she was gloriously naked. Her body was full and firm, and he could feel the heat from her. She came to him again and they kissed. This time his hands roamed over her, finally settling on her buttocks, which were round and solid.

She broke the kiss again and began kissing his chest. She worked her way down to his belly, going to her knees to do so. Finally, she undid his belt and his trousers and pulled them down to his ankles. When she tugged his underwear down, his erection popped into view, full and pulsating.

"Mmmm," she said, touching him. She slid her fingers up the underside of his penis with one hand while cradling his testicles with the other. Then she closed her hand around him and began to glide up and down, rubbing him, pulling on him.

"Jesse—" he said warningly.

"Shhh," she said, "I know what to do."

And she did. Still holding him she began to cover him with wet kisses, "umming" and "oohing" as she did so. She ran her tongue up along the underside of him and found that tender place just beneath the head of his penis. He jerked as her tongue touched him, and then she was avidly licking the head of his cock, which was growing almost purple as it became more and more engorged.

"Mmm," she said, "it looks like a luscious plum."

And so saying she took him into her mouth, sucking first on the head, making it very wet, and then taking more of him into her mouth, and more, and then she started bobbing up and down on him, sucking him. All the while the scent of her filled his nostrils, not just the perfume but her natural scent as her excitement heightened and she became wetter and wetter.

She fondled his testicles as she sucked him, and then slid both hands around to cup his buttocks as she took him deeper and deeper into her mouth.

"Jesse—" he said, wanting to warn her, but she ignored him and continued to suck him. She slid one finger down along the crease between his ass cheeks. She found his anus and touched it gently, sucking him with more and more eagerness. Finally, he could hold back no longer and he exploded into her mouth. Her eyes widened, and then closed as she took all of him in. When he was empty she withdrew him from her mouth and licked the head some more before smiling up at him.

"That was a good start," she said.

"Don't you have to go back—"

"He's a sound sleeper," she said, still holding his penis and fondling it. "You didn't go completely soft. That's a good sign. It means you're interested in me."

"I think we should move to the bed," he told her, "and I'll show you just how interested I am."

ELEVEN

Clint found Jessica McCrain to be a formidable opponent in bed—and that seemed to be the way she treated sex, like a contest that had to be won.

As well as being solidly built she was also very strong. At one point during the next several hours he had her pinned down on her back while he was lying between her legs, returning the favor. He was avidly working on her with his mouth and tongue, and as she neared orgasm she suddenly tried to get out from under him.

"Oh, God," she moaned, "you're going to kill me," and proceeded to try to push him away from her. When that didn't work she tried rolling over and it took all his strength to keep her from doing so.

"God, oh, God," she gasped, trying to keep her voice down. At one point she even started beating on his shoulders, but he was determined not to stop until she was ready to scream. Of course, if she did scream it would bring the whole house down on them, but he wasn't thinking about that at the moment.

He felt her go rigid, and then her belly started to tremble. He kept licking her until she lifted her butt up off the bed, made a sound that to anyone listening outside the door would sound as if she were trying to lift some great weight, and then she was thrashing about beneath him. He finally took his mouth off of her, but before she could stop him he was on her, and then in her. He slid in so easily because she was very wet, and he began to take her in long, hard strokes while she wrapped her arms and legs around him and sank her teeth into his shoulder in an effort not to scream.

"What were you trying to do?" she asked afterward, still out of breath, "bring the whole house down on us? God, it was all I could do not to scream!"

"I know," he said, touching the tender spot on his shoulder.

"I'm sorry," she said, "but it's your fault. I mean—God, a man has never done that to me before."

"A man has never . . . kissed you there?"

"Kissed, yes," she said, touching herself between her legs, "but not . . . that! Not what you did. You made me lose control."

"And you've never lost control before."

"No," she said, shaking her head. "Not with a man."

She got up from the bed then and started looking for her nightgown and robe.

"Leaving?" he asked.

"Oh, yes," she said. "I have to think about this." She turned to face him, wearing her nightgown and robe. "You've changed the way I think about men."

"What's wrong with that?"

"That's what I have to decide," she said. "Whether or not this is a good thing."

"Didn't I give you pleasure?"

"That's just it," she said. "I'm used to giving, not receiving. I've been giving men pleasure for so long, without getting any back, that I made a game of it. It became a power I had over them. This . . . what happened here tonight . . . changes everything."

"You mean . . . I've ruined everything for you?"

"That just might be the conclusion I come to," she said,

moving toward the door, "but right now all I know is I have to think about it."

With that she went out the door, leaving Clint totally amazed, and confused. Never before had a woman *complained* so about being given pleasure, or been so totally confused by receiving it.

This just might go down in history as his most amazing sexual encounter with a woman, and not only because Jesse McCrain had a splendid body and a voracious appetite.

She just might turn out to be the most confusing woman he'd ever met.

TWELVE

Apparently Jessica McCrain had not come to any decisions overnight and was still confused by what had happened, because at breakfast she did not speak to or look at Clint. Likewise, Gerald McCrain paid Clint no mind. Had he awakened during the night to find his wife gone? Had he assumed she went to Clint's room? Or was he simply being rude? Clint thought it was probably the last.

As with dinner the male occupants of the other rooms were not present.

"Our friend, the scientist, left early this morning," Henry Van Allen said.

Clint and Henry had checked the night before and found that the scientist's name was William Kent, and he had been on the island, at Van Allen's inn, for the past three years at this time. That cleared him of the murders committed during the first two years, which probably cleared him altogether.

The other man, however, was named Bradshaw—first initial T.—and he had never been to the inn before. What they did not know was whether or not he had ever been to the island before

"Did you see him?" Clint asked.

"No, but Mrs. Livingstone did. She gave him some coffee."

"I should speak with her about him," Clint said. "I'll

do it after lunch. Now what about this Bradshaw? You said he takes all his meals in his room?''

''Yes,'' Van Allen said. ''Mrs. Livingstone takes up a tray and leaves it outside the door. Then she goes up and collects the tray later.''

''That means he has to open and close the door and reach outside at least six times a day. Someone must have seen him, in all this time.''

''I'm sorry,'' Mary Morgan said from Clint's left, ''but are you talking about Mr. Bradshaw? I couldn't help overhearing.''

''Yes, we are.''

''I've seen him.''

''You have?'' Clint asked.

''Well,'' she said, qualifying her statement, ''I've seen his arms and the back of his head. Our room is right down the hall from his.''

''You haven't seen his face?'' Clint asked.

''No,'' she said, ''although I did see his profile once.''

''Is his face scarred?''

She thought a moment.

''It was his left profile, and his skin didn't seem scarred.''

''Would you recognize him if you saw him?''

She shook her head. ''I doubt it. Why? Why are you curious about him?''

''That's just it,'' Clint said. ''I'm curious about a man who never leaves his room.''

''Do you suspect him of something?''

''Like what?'' Clint asked.

''I don't know,'' she said. ''You just don't seem like the kind of man who would be curious about someone like Mr. Bradshaw without a good reason.''

''Maybe he thinks this Bradshaw is the man who has been killing these girls,'' McCrain said.

They all looked at McCrain.

"Is that what you think, Mr. McCrain?" Henry Van Allen asked.

"I don't have any thoughts on the subject," McCrain said.

"You must," Van Allen said, "or else why would you have made that comment? Or are you just trying to start a rumor?"

"I don't start rumors, Captain," McCrain said. "Like Adams, here, I've been curious about the man. Maybe he goes out at night when nobody can see him?"

"I don't think so," Mary Morgan said.

"Why?" McCrain asked.

"Because Mother's never heard him go out," Mary said, "and she is usually in our room, and always in the room at night."

"He could sneak out without her knowing it."

"I don't think so," Mary said, and then looked at Van Allen. "Captain, I'm afraid the floor outside our rooms creaks rather loudly."

Van Allen smiled and said, "It's an old building."

"He could still get out when everyone's asleep," McCrain maintained. "I'm just saying it's a possibility, that's all."

"Aren't you worried about this killer, Mr. McCrain?" Clint asked. "Doesn't his presence make you want to leave the island?"

"Ha!" McCrain said. "I wanted to leave the day we got here. In fact, I never wanted to come at all."

He looked at his wife then, as if expecting her to make some remark, and he looked surprised that she did not. Jessica McCrain continued to stare into her plate as she ate her eggs and bacon, or smeared marmalade onto a piece of bread.

"Why don't you just leave the poor man alone?" Julia Morgan asked. "He's not harming anyone by wanting to stay in his room. Why suspect him of anything?"

"Someone has to be suspect," McCrain said. "You women are being killed."

"Aren't you worried about your wife when she goes outside alone?" Van Allen asked.

"My wife is not a young woman," McCrain said. "It seems to me this young woman here—" he indicated Mary Morgan with a slight incline of his head—"would be more worried."

He looked at his wife again, as if he'd been baiting her and expected her to rise to it—which she didn't. Clint was even more puzzled by her reaction to having sex with him. He'd never had this effect on a woman before.

"Why should I be worried?" Mary asked.

"His victims are attractive young women, as I understand it," McCrain said.

"My daughter does not think of herself as attractive," Julia Morgan said.

"Why, that's ridiculous," Captain Van Allen said. "She's extremely pretty."

"You'll never convince her of that," Julia said.

Mary remained quiet while the others talked about her.

"I don't understand," Van Allen said.

"Let it go, Henry," Clint said, giving his friend a look.

"But—"

Clint shook his head, and Van Allen subsided and allowed the subject to drop.

After breakfast, as the others went off to do whatever they were going to do that day, Clint said to Van Allen, "I want to go and see the police chief. Can you give me directions?"

"I can do better than that," Van Allen said. "I can walk you there."

"Directions will be good enough," Clint said. "I want to take a look at the town, anyway."

"All right," Van Allen said, and gave Clint what he wanted.

"And can you tell me where this scientist is doing his research?"

"As a matter of fact," Van Allen said, "he mentioned something this morning to Mrs. Livingstone about Arch Rock. Maybe you and Mrs. McCrain should go there together."

"Somehow," Clint said to his friend, "I think Mrs. McCrain has lost her interest in Arch Rock."

THIRTEEN

Following Van Allen's directions Clint walked from the inn to the town. The main street was lined with restaurants and shops of all kinds, and it was further down, past the ferry stop, where he found the police station. It was a two-story brick building that looked like the newest building on the block.

He entered and found himself in a huge room with a high ceiling. There was a stairway going up to a second floor, but he couldn't see where it went, or what was up there. In the back, against the wall, was a desk, and Chief of Police Anson Stewart was seated there. When the door closed behind Clint, the chief looked up from his desk.

"Mr. Adams. Good morning."

"Good morning, Chief."

"Please, come in."

As Clint approached the chief, he saw that the man's desk was encircled by a low fence, with entry through a swinging door. Clint went through the door and Stewart waved him to a chair. Stewart was wearing a regular suit today, not a uniform.

"Coffee?"

"Yes, thanks."

"I always keep a pot going."

He turned around and plucked the pot off of a stove, poured two cups and handed Clint one.

"What brings you down here so early?" Stewart asked.

"The inn serves breakfast early."

"Oh, yeah, so they do."

"Chief, are you nervous about something?"

Stewart leaned back in his chair.

"I had a visit from the mayor this morning," Stewart said. "As I suspected, my job is on the line. Stop this killer this time, or I won't be here next year when he comes back."

"Well, you just said you suspected this would happen. In fact, last night you were wondering why it hadn't happened sooner."

"So I was—but when it really happens it sort of, you know, hits you."

"Then I guess we'd better get started if I'm going to help," Clint said. "Can you show me where the two girls were found?"

"Sure."

"And have you talked to the other hotels in town about our two friends from Captain Van Allen's inn?"

"Not yet."

"Well, you'd better do that today," Clint said. "We've established that the scientist fella has been here the past three years."

"Not the first two?"

"Not at Van Allen's," Clint said, "but maybe at one of the other hotels."

Stewart sat straight up in his chair.

"If he was here all five years then he's—"

"A good suspect," Clint said. "Let's not jump to conclusions, Chief. Let's just see if we can talk to these fellas."

"All right," Chief Stewart said, standing up, "the other hotels and inns first, then."

"Including the big one."

"The big one?"

"What's it called? The Grand Hotel?"

Stewart hesitated.

"The Grand Hotel?"

"Well, sure," Clint said, "maybe one of these fellas stayed there four or five years ago. What's the matter? Haven't you ever been up there?"

"Well, actually, no," Stewart said.

"What do they do if they need a policeman?"

"I believe they handle all of their problems themselves."

"And back when the first girls were killed? You never checked up there?"

"No."

"And each year, when the girls were killed?"

"No."

"Chief," Clint said, "were you told not to bother those people up there?"

"Well," Stewart said, "actually, yes."

"By whom?"

"By the mayor," Stewart said. "See, a lot of the guests from that hotel come down here and shop, and sometimes eat. The mayor didn't want me rocking the boat, so to speak."

"Did he think that just by going up there and asking a few questions you would close that place down?"

"Well, of course not—"

"Chief," Clint said, "if you want my help we have to go up there and talk to somebody."

"Can we do it discreetly?" Stewart asked.

"I think we can do that."

"Maybe we should talk to the mayor."

"And give him a chance to stop us?" Clint asked. "Haven't you ever wanted to go up there and ask questions, Chief?"

"Well, of course . . ."

"Here's your chance," Clint said. "You're not going to let your chance pass you by, are you?"

Chief Stewart thought it over for a few moments, then said, "No . . . no, I'm not."

"Then let's go."

FOURTEEN

The Grand Hotel was the most luxurious building Clint had ever seen. There was nothing in New York or San Francisco he knew of that could match its grandeur. There were people sitting outside on a porch that wrapped around, and when they entered the hotel the lobby was large enough to hold a baseball game in.

"Wow," Clint said.

He glanced at Stewart, who was looking around the place with an unhappy expression on his face. It took Clint a moment to realize that the man was terribly intimidated.

"We should probably ask for the manager," Clint said.

"Oh, yes," Stewart said.

"Let's try that desk over there."

Clint led the way to an unmarked desk with a man standing behind it.

"Excuse me?" Clint said.

The man looked up from whatever he'd been doing and looked both Stewart and Clint up and down.

"You are not guests," he said.

"You can tell that just by looking at us, can you?" Clint asked.

"Yes, sir," the man said, almost with a sneer. "Can I help you?" He was in his thirties and had a severely superior attitude that was rubbing Clint the wrong way.

"I doubt it," Clint said.

"Why is that?"

"Because you're not the manager of this hotel."

"And how do you know that?"

Clint grinned.

"I can tell just by looking at you."

The man didn't like that, but before he could say anything Chief Stewart produced his badge.

"Get the manager."

"Is there a problem?" the man asked.

"Yes," Clint said. "You're not getting the manager."

The man stared at them for a few moments, but he wilted trying to match looks with both of them.

"Excuse me."

Clint was glad that the chief had backed his play, despite being intimidated by his surroundings.

"That was fun," Stewart said, and when Clint looked at him the man seemed more relaxed.

"They're just people," Clint said, and then added, "with a lot of money."

"I know," Stewart said.

The snide man returned with an older gentleman who had a perplexed look on his face. He was in his fifties, with black hair streaked with silver and a carefully trimmed mustache.

"Gentlemen," he said, "was there something my assistant couldn't help you with?"

"Yes," Clint said, "he couldn't seem to locate his manners."

Now the manager frowned.

"I see," he said. "My name is Claude DuVallier, I am the manager of the Grand Hotel. And you gentlemen are?"

"My name is Stewart, Mr. DuVallier," the chief said. He displayed his badge and identification. "I am the chief of police of Mackinac Island."

"I see." DuVallier then looked pointedly at Clint. "And this gentleman is?"

"My associate."

DuVallier seemed to be waiting for something further and when it didn't come he cleared his throat.

"Perhaps you gentlemen should come to my office," he said finally.

"Lead on, Mr. DuVallier," Stewart said, "we'll be right behind you."

As they walked past the assistant manager—whose name they still didn't know—the man gave Clint a look that he was tempted to return by sticking his tongue out at him.

Instead, he ignored him and followed Chief Stewart and Claude DuVallier.

When they reached the manager's office he invited them to sit and seated himself behind a long but slender mahogany desk, the top of which was totally bare.

"I apologize if you found my assistant manager's manners lacking," DuVallier said.

"As a matter of fact," Stewart said, surprising Clint with his sudden turnaround, "I found them appalling."

"I see," DuVallier said, then cleared his throat again. "I shall have to talk to him about that, won't I?"

"I would hope so."

"Yes . . . well, what can I do for you gentlemen?"

"We are investigating a string of murders, Mr. DuVallier."

"A string of murders. How terrible—oh, I think I see—are you speaking of the . . . the young women who have been killed these past . . . four years, is it?"

"Five," Stewart corrected him.

"Yes, five . . . and after five years what has brought you to the Grand Hotel?"

"We're looking at two suspects, sir, and what we need to know from you is whether or not they have ever been guests here at the Grand Hotel."

"I see," DuVallier said. It seemed to be his favorite phrase. Clint wondered if he really did "see" each time he said it. "I must tell you we treat our guests' privacy with the utmost respect, Chief."

"I realize that, Mr. DuVallier," the chief said. "I wouldn't ask you if it wasn't a matter of murder. You understand, I'm sure."

DuVallier stared at the chief for a few seconds, with the chief staring right back. Finally, the Grand Hotel manager sighed.

"Very well," he said. "Have you the names written down?"

"No, we don't . . ." Stewart said, and Clint knew the man was on the verge of being embarrassed.

"But that's easily remedied," he broke in. "May I have a paper and pencil?"

"Surely."

DuVallier pushed the items across the table and it was Chief Stewart who wrote the names of Captain Henry Van Allen's two mysterious male guests.

"There," he said, pushing the paper back.

"I can't do this right now," the man said, "not immediately. I'll have to have someone go through the records, and that will take some time."

"Not too much time, I hope," Stewart said. "I'd like to wrap this up before this man kills another woman."

"Do you think you can?" the manager asked. "Catch him, I mean, after all this time?"

"We're going to do our best," Stewart said, "but we need your help."

"Of course," DuVallier said. "I'll have someone get to it right away. When I have an answer I'll have it run down to you at the police station. Is that satisfactory?"

Chief Stewart stood up and said, "Very."

DuVallier stood and extended his hand. "We are glad to assist the police in their inquiries."

"Thank you, sir."

Clint nodded to the manager and said, "Thank you," then followed Chief Stewart out of the office and out of the building. The chief began to move faster and faster as he approached the door and only stopped when he was out on the porch.

Clint caught up to him and saw that the man was sweating and gasping for breath.

"Are you all right?" Clint asked.

The chief nodded.

"They're just people," he said, "only with more money than us."

"Right," Clint said. "Come on, let's get you away from here."

FIFTEEN

They went back down to Mackinac and found a bar. When they were seated at a table with a cold beer before each of them the chief finally seemed to be able to control his anxiety.

"Now you know why I don't go up there," Stewart said.

"Heights?"

Stewart laughed.

"I wish it was that simple," he said. "Those people scare the hell out of me."

"Which people are those, Chief?"

"Rich people."

"Oh, Chief," Clint said, "you picked the wrong profession if you're scared of rich people. They'll use that against you."

"Don't you think I know that?" Stewart asked. "How do you think I ended up on this island? Do you know how many jobs I've had in law enforcement? How many jobs I've *lost* in law enforcement because I couldn't stand up to some rich bastard?"

"I know all about it, Chief," Clint said. "That's one of the reasons I left law enforcement years ago."

"I tried that," he said, "but I couldn't stay away. I always ended up running for office somewhere and, somehow, winning. I'd pin on the badge, things would go all right for a while, and then some rich bastard would come walking into my office asking for a favor."

"And then another?"

Stewart nodded and said, "And still another."

"So that's why you haven't gone up to the Grand Hotel all these years?"

"That's right," Stewart said.

"Why now, then?" Clint asked. "Not because I forced you?"

"No," Stewart said, "no, I guess I've just decided to find out if, by not going up there for the past five years, I've managed to get a lot of young women killed."

"Oh, now, I don't think you ought to take the blame for that, Chief. There's somebody else out there deserves the blame more than you do."

"Most of the blame, yes," Stewart said, "but maybe I'm the one who's been letting him get away with it, maybe all because I couldn't do what I did today."

"Well, that remains to be seen, I guess," Clint said, "but there's no point in beating yourself up with it now, is there?"

"No, I guess not."

They both finished their beers and stood up.

"Are you okay?" Clint asked.

"Yes," Stewart said, "my heart rate is back to normal, and I'm not sweating anymore. You know, sometimes I don't think it's anxiety that brings it on."

"No? What then?"

"Anger," Stewart said. "Pure, unadulterated anger—and sometimes I'm afraid I'll lose control of it."

"You won't."

"No? What makes you say that?"

"Because you're a professional."

Stewart snorted.

"No, I mean it," Clint said. "You're a born lawman, Stewart. Just look at the way you can't stay away from it.

I walked away from it, you can't. This is what you were meant to be."

"Oh, I don't think—"

"This," Clint said, touching Stewart's breast pocket where he was keeping his badge, "is what you are meant to be doing. I've seen many lawmen in my time."

"You don't even know me."

"Believe me," Clint said, "I've seen and heard enough to know what I'm talking about."

"Really?"

"Yes."

"Well . . . maybe you're right."

"I know I am."

Stewart seemed to draw himself up, actually become an inch or so taller.

"Come on," the chief said, "let's go and check out the other hotels and inns in town."

"I'm right behind you, Chief," Clint said as they headed for the door.

SIXTEEN

Clint followed Stewart around for the rest of the day, letting the chief do all of the talking at the other hotels and inns on the island. In the end, they came up empty. Neither of the men they were interested in had ever stayed at those places.

"That just leaves the Grand Hotel," Anson Stewart said over dinner. He'd promised Clint that there was a restaurant on the island that made a great steak, and he was right. It came with all the trimmings, and a pot of hot, black coffee.

"This kind of meal could keep me here longer," Clint said.

"How long were you planning to stay?" Stewart asked.

"Before I agreed to help find a killer?" Clint asked. "I'm not even sure. It was a couple of years ago when Henry invited me. All I knew was that I was coming to see his inn, and the island."

"Well, you've seen his inn, and some of the island," Stewart said, "but there's plenty more to see."

"So I understand," Clint said. "Like Arch Rock."

"Exactly."

"You know," Clint said, "I think that scientist is doing some tests out there. I think I'll go and talk to him tomorrow."

"That's a good idea," Stewart said. "You could make

it look like you were just taking a look at the rock formation.''

''I could do that,'' Clint said, nodding. ''Yeah, I think I will.''

''And what about the other one?'' Stewart asked. ''The one who won't come out of his room.''

''Well,'' Clint said, ''you could break the door down.''

''I don't want to do that,'' Stewart said. ''Not unless I've got evidence that he's the one.''

''Well, then, let me concentrate on the scientist,'' Clint said. ''At least we know that he was on the island the last three years.''

''We just need to place him here the other two.''

They finished their meals and lingered over peach pie and more coffee.

''Mrs. Livingstone is going to be mad you missed her dinner tonight,'' Stewart said.

''I'll say I was detained by the chief of police.''

''You know,'' Stewart said, ''I really have to thank you for what you did today.''

''All I did was follow you around all day.''

''Not in the beginning,'' Stewart said. ''I mean this morning, at the Grand. You got me there, you spoke up, you *showed* me they were like anybody else. I mean, the way that pompous ass talked to us in the beginning—''

''Hey,'' Clint said, ''you picked right up on it, and backed me up—and after that you took charge. You did great.''

''Well,'' Stewart said, ''I still don't think I could have done it without you. Thanks again.''

''Sure, Chief,'' Clint said. ''Anytime.''

They left the restaurant and stopped on the street out front.

''You aren't getting your men in on this?'' Clint asked. ''I mean, we checked the hotels ourselves.''

''I've got them on patrol.''

"That's funny," Clint said. "I haven't seen them all day."

"They're patrolling the island, not the streets," Stewart said. "I've got them on the lookout for young women walking alone, or with a fella. You know, young lovers looking for a place to be together?"

"Has that happened before?" Clint asked. "Women being attacked even though they're with a man?"

"No," Stewart said, "but I don't want to take any chances."

"Can't say I blame you for that. Say, you were going to show me where the two women were killed."

Stewart looked up at the sky.

"Better to do that in daylight, and it's going to be dark soon. Tomorrow?"

"I'll be at your office after breakfast," Clint said. "Good night."

"Good night, Clint, and thanks again."

When Clint got back to the inn Captain Van Allen was sitting on the porch.

"Wouldn't go in if I was you," he said to Clint.

"Mrs. Livingstone?"

The older man nodded.

"Says she made tonight's dinner just for you."

Clint settled into a chair next to Van Allen's. From his vantage point he could see the lights going on in the sanitarium.

"What kind of people they got in there?" he asked.

"Sick people."

"Crazy people?"

"I don't think so," Van Allen said. "I've heard that Doc Holliday went to a place like that after Tombstone."

"I heard that, too," Clint said. "So that's the kind of place it is?"

"I don't know for sure, Clint."

"Well," Clint said, "maybe somebody should find out."

SEVENTEEN

The night turned out to be uneventful for Clint. He got to his room without running into Mrs. Livingstone, and Jessica McCrain didn't come to see him. The latter was a kind of good news, bad news situation, but he accepted it and went to sleep.

The next morning Mrs. Livingstone served Clint his breakfast in stony silence. Of course, this was the way she usually served the meals, so no one noticed anything. Clint was the only one who felt the chill.

"What's on the agenda for today?" Captain Van Allen asked.

"Chief Stewart is going to show me where the two women were found."

"What good will that do?"

"There might be something on the ground that will help."

"Like what?"

"Sign."

"Ah," Van Allen said, "we're being very Western today, aren't we?"

"Do you remember the river captain you met on the Mississippi?"

"Very well."

"He could read the river the way some men can read the

ground,'' Clint said. ''You were impressed with him.''

''Yes, I was,'' Van Allen said. ''I apologize—but can you read the ground that well?''

''Better than anyone else on this island, I'll bet,'' Clint said.

''And then what?''

''I don't know,'' Clint said, wiping his mouth with his napkin and pushing his chair back. ''I guess we'll just have to wait and see what the ground yields.''

Chief Stewart maintained a respectful silence while Clint studied the ground of both locations for some sort of sign. He didn't speak until Clint stood up from the ground of the second location.

''Pretty foolish of them to be out here,'' Stewart said. Both locations were away from the town and isolated.

''They didn't come out on their own, Chief.''

''You mean they were carried?''

''Dragged,'' Clint said. ''Look here.''

The chief moved in for a look and Clint showed him the drag marks on the ground.

''Those are from her heels,'' Clint said. ''The same marks were at the other location.''

''I'll be damned,'' Stewart said. ''I didn't see that.''

''No reason you should have if you're not trained to,'' Clint said.

''Is there anything else here?''

''As a matter of fact, there is.''

''Like what?''

''Like the killer's signature.''

''What?''

''I'll show you.''

They walked to another spot where Clint knelt down on one knee and Stewart did the same. Clint pointed to the ground.

''That's a footprint.''

Stewart stared at what seemed to him to be hard-packed dirt.

"I don't see it."

"Trust me," Clint said. "It's there."

"What about it?"

"The right heel has a nick," Clint said. "That's like leaving a signature." Clint stood up and brushed his hands off.

"I don't get it."

"All we have to do," Clint explained patiently, "is find those boots, and you'll have your killer—unless there are two or more men sharing the same boots."

"Goddamn," Stewart said. "You've got to show me how to do that."

"Lessons later," Clint said. "Right now I want to go to Arch Rock and meet William Kent, our scientist friend."

"I'll come, too."

"I don't think that's a good idea," Clint said. "I can't very well claim to have accidentally found it if I show up with the police chief."

"You have a point there."

"I'll walk back to town with you," Clint said.

During the walk Stewart said, "I can't start checking every pair of boots in town. How do we do this?"

"Well," Clint said, "we can start by checking the boots of Kent and Bradshaw."

"But Bradshaw won't come out of his room."

"We'll have to figure out a way to get a look at his boots," Clint said, "but I can get a look at Kent's at Arch Rock."

"And what should I do in the meantime?"

"Why don't you see if you can get us into that sanitarium."

"That place? Why?"

"Have you checked out their security?"

"No," Stewart said, "I have to admit I haven't been up there."

"Same reason as the Grand Hotel?"

"Sort of," Stewart said, "but not as bad."

"You were told to leave them alone, too?"

"That's right."

"Why do I get the feeling the mayor of this town isn't going to be too happy with you if we don't find this killer?"

"My job's already on the line," Stewart said. "He can't fire me more than once . . . can he?"

EIGHTEEN

Clint found his way to Arch Rock and stood in awe of the natural formation. It was certainly large enough for a man to walk through, and to him looked more like a crude circle than an arch. He walked around it so that when he looked through it he could see the Straits of Mackinac. He wondered idly if this was not a natural formation but man-made, having to do perhaps with defense of the island, or something totally different. He was wondering what it would be like to walk through the arch and perhaps be transported somewhere else, someplace far away, maybe not even on this world when a man spoke from behind him. He'd known someone was there because he'd heard the sound of a boot scraping over rock, but he had not sensed any danger.

"Breathtaking, isn't it?"

He turned in the direction of the voice and saw a man standing there.

"It certainly is."

"What were you thinking, staring at it that way?"

"You'd laugh."

"No, I won't," the man said. He was in his thirties, tall but very slender, with dark, curly hair.

Clint told him what he'd been thinking, holding nothing back, and the man listened with great interest.

"And now you can laugh," Clint finished.

"But I won't," the man said. "I don't want to. You see, I am a scientist, and what you've told me does not sound as far-fetched as you might think."

"Oh, come on," Clint said. "How could you be sent someplace else simply by walking through an arch?"

"Who knows what the future holds?" the man asked. "There could be any number of modes of travel that we haven't discovered yet."

"Well," Clint said, "I think I'll stick to the tried-and-true."

"And they are?"

"Foot," Clint said, "or horseback."

"Oh, come now," the man said. "Certainly to get here you used more than that."

"Well . . . I did travel part of the way by rail."

"And then by ferry to get to the island."

"Yes."

"You see?" the man said. "Tried-and-true will not always get you there."

Clint came down from the precipice and walked up to the dark-haired man.

"My name is Kent," the scientist said, extending his hand. "William Kent—Bill, if you like."

"Clint Adams," Clint said, shaking the man's hand. "Happy to meet you."

"What brings you to the arch?" Kent asked.

"I was just wandering around, actually," Clint said. "When I saw this I just had to have a closer look."

"Can't say that I blame you."

Both men stood and stared at the formation for a few moments.

"What about you?" Clint asked.

"What do you mean?"

"What brings you here?"

"Oh, I've been all over the island," the man said. "Yesterday, today, and tomorrow I'll be here, and then I'll move on."

"Doing some kind of work?" Clint asked.

"Of course," Kent said, but did not elaborate.

"I'm staying at the inn owned by Captain Henry Van Allen," Clint said. "Maybe I can buy you a drink later."

"I'm sure you could," the man said, smiling. "You see, I, too, am staying there."

"Really?" Clint said. "That's odd. I haven't see you there but—wait. There's supposed to be a mysterious man staying in one of the rooms. Would that be you?"

Kent laughed.

"I'd hardly call myself mysterious," Kent said. "No, it's not me, but I know who you mean. A fellow named Bradshaw who never comes out of his room."

"That's him," Clint said. "Do you know him?"

"I've never seen him," Kent said.

"Well, I still haven't seen you there, certainly not at mealtimes."

"I take my meals with me," Kent said, patting a leather bag that he carried over his shoulder. "I have no time, I'm afraid, for the pleasantries of eating with the other guests."

"Well, that answers my questions, then," Clint said. "I've often wondered about the empty chairs at mealtimes."

"I generally leave the house very early," Kent said, "and return late each night."

"You can't be getting much sleep then."

"I don't need much."

"And what about food? Surely you need to eat better than you are."

"Mrs. Livingstone is quite generous each day," Kent said.

"What have you done to deserve that kind of treatment?" Clint asked.

"I've stayed at the inn for three years in a row now," Kent said. "I'm a regular. The old girl and I talk quite a bit. I think she likes me."

"I see."

"And I'm afraid I've spent too much time talking," Kent said. "There's work to be done."

"But I—"

"Perhaps we can have that drink one day soon, Clint," Kent said, and simply walked off, his pace brisk, before Clint could say another word.

NINETEEN

Clint walked back to the inn, realizing all the way that he'd learned virtually nothing about what kind of scientist William Kent was. Still, that really didn't matter as much as finding out if the man was on the island the first two years that the women had been killed—and he hadn't had a chance to do that, either. Now that he'd met the man, however, he was going to make a point of "running into him" again, this time at the inn.

The only way to do that, though, was to get up when he got up, and manage to be in the area of the kitchen when he got his food from Mrs. Livingstone. That meant getting back into the woman's good graces.

Clint managed to find some wildflowers on the way back and picked them to give to Mrs. Livingstone. When he reached the inn Mary Morgan was sitting out on the porch.

"And who is the lucky recipient of those?" she asked as he mounted the porch.

"They're for Mrs. Livingstone," Clint said.

"Ah, that's right," Mary said, "you missed dinner last night."

"Yes, I did," he said. "These are a peace offering."

"Well, flowers usually work on women," Mary said.

"I hope they work on this one."

"I noticed you coming from that direction," Mary said, pointing. "Did you manage to see Arch Rock?"

"As a matter of fact I did," Clint said. "I also met our elusive neighbor, Mr. Kent."

"The scientist."

"Yes."

"What's he like?" she asked anxiously. "I've been dying to meet him."

"Well, he's young, very pleasant-looking—"

"I don't want to marry him, Clint," she said, "I've just been wanting to meet him, to see what kind of man he is."

"Well, he was very pleasant, not as standoffish as I thought he'd be, given his tendency to avoid all of us."

"That's odd," she said.

"I thought so, too."

"What else?"

"Well," Clint said, "he was very talkative and was as in awe of Arch Rock as I was, even though I'm sure he had seen it before."

"I've seen it several times myself," Mary Morgan said, "and I'm still in awe. Do you think he'll be out by the rock again tomorrow?"

"I'm sure he will be."

She clapped her hands together once and said, "I think I'll pretend to run into him there by accident."

Not bothering to tell her that he had done that very thing today, Clint said, "You're a very devious woman, Miss Morgan."

"Thank you, Mr. Adams."

"Now I think I'll get these to Mrs. Livingstone before they wilt."

"Sounds like a good idea."

"Maybe I should get some more and bring them to your mother."

Mary stared up at him, surprised.

"Why would you do that?"

"I think she could use a man bringing her flowers, don't you?"

"As a matter of fact," Mary said, "I do. I think that would be very nice, except for one thing."

"What's that?"

"She thinks you're the type of man who would bring her flowers and then want something from her."

Clint frowned. "She thinks all men are that type, doesn't she?"

"Yes, she does."

"Except your father?"

"Oh, no," Mary said, "she knew he was the type, too. Believe me, she loved my father a lot, but she wouldn't want another man like him."

"And she thinks all men are like him?"

"Right."

"It doesn't seem as if she'd give a man a chance to prove otherwise."

"No, it doesn't."

"Then it seems as if I should just forget the idea of giving her flowers."

"Unless you want to be the man who tries to change her mind."

"Your mother is an attractive woman, Mary," he said, "but to tell you the truth I don't think I have the time to do that right now."

"You're helping the police with their investigation into the death of those women, aren't you?"

"Yes, I am."

"I know your reputation, Clint," she said. "I don't remember anything about you being a detective."

"I'm not," he said, "but I have worked with some, men like Allan Pinkerton and Talbot Roper."

"I've heard of both of them," she said, impressed. "They're famous."

"Yes, they are," he said, "and maybe I've learned just a little bit from them that might be helpful here."

"Well, for the sake of everyone involved," she said, "I hope so."

TWENTY

Mrs. Livingstone was like most women Clint had ever known. As he handed her the flowers she melted and forgave him, and in the next breath she told him what she'd do to him if he missed one of her dinners again.

"Now that you've forgiven me," he said then, "I would like to ask you a question."

"About what?" she asked, placing the flowers in water.

"One of the guests here."

"Who would that be?" She turned to face him, drying her hands on her apron.

"William Kent."

"What about him?" she asked. "I'm not supposed to talk about the guests."

"Well, I know that you prepare food for him every day to take with him when he leaves."

"The captain said it was all right."

"I'm not questioning that, Mrs. Livingstone," Clint said. "What I wanted to know was what you thought of the man."

"I think he's a nice man," she said.

"He told me he was a regular here."

"This is the third year he's stayed here," she said. "I suppose that makes him a regular."

"I guess it does," Clint said. "Do you know if he was ever on the island before that?"

"How would I know that?" she asked. "If he didn't stay here, how would I know?"

She seemed too defensive to him, but he didn't want to attack her.

"I thought perhaps, when you were talking with him, that he might have mentioned it."

"We don't talk that much," she said. "I just fix him the food because the captain tells me to."

"Like with Mr. Bradshaw?"

"That's right."

Kent had told Clint that he and "the old girl" talked quite a bit. Why was she lying about it? To protect him? And what did she think he needed protection from?

"I have to get back to work now," she said.

"Of course. I'm sorry I took up so much of your time, Mrs. Livingstone."

"That's all right," she said, "and thank you again for the flowers."

"You're welcome."

He left the kitchen then and went out to the sitting room. There he saw Gerald McCrain sitting on one of the sofas reading a newspaper. At first he thought he'd avoid the man, but at the last minute he changed his mind. McCrain was opinionated self-important, but maybe he knew something useful.

"Good afternoon," Clint said, entering the room.

McCrain lowered his newspaper with a curious expression on his face, which turned to distaste when he saw Clint.

"Good afternoon, Adams."

"Do you mind if I sit?"

"This sitting room is available to all guests," McCrain said. "Guess I couldn't stop you if I wanted to."

Clint figured that was as much of an invitation as he was going to get and sat on another sofa.

"If you don't mind me saying," Clint said, "I was interested in what you had to say about the women who have been killed.''

The man lowered his paper again and stared at Clint.

''Why would you be interested in what I had to say?''

''You're a successful businessman, Mr. McCrain,'' Clint said. ''Something like that doesn't happen by accident. That means you're also an intelligent man.''

''Well,'' McCrain said, the paper falling further, ''yes . . .''

''Who do you think is killing these women?''

Now he set the newspaper down in his lap and gave Clint his full attention.

''Well, I don't know who did it, mind you,'' McCrain said, ''but I do know one thing.''

''What's that?''

''The chief of police they have here is not going to solvc it.''

''Why do you say that?''

''He was on the Pittsburgh Police Department for a short time,'' McCrain said, ''until they fired him.''

''And why did they do that?''

''Because he was a drunk.''

Clint and Chief Stewart had had a beer together, and the man didn't strike him as a drunk.

''He was also crooked.''

''When was this, Mr. McCrain?''

''About ten years ago,'' McCrain said.

''And you remember?''

''I remember him,'' the man said, ''but apparently he doesn't remember me.''

''Had you ever met in Pittsburgh?''

''Actually, no, we hadn't, but I had seen him there, and I remember his name.''

''And were you the successful businessman you are now?'' Clint asked.

''Not as successful, no.''

''Well, then,'' Clint said, realizing he'd made a mistake,

"maybe there's just no reason he should remember you."

He stood up. If McCrain was going to bad-mouth Stewart then the man had nothing important to add.

"I thought you wanted my opinion?" McCrain said.

Clint fixed the man with a hard stare and said, "I've changed my mind," and left the room.

TWENTY-ONE

Clint started back to his own room but to get there he had to pass the Bradshaw room. He stopped short and knocked impulsively.

There was no answer.

He knocked again, but still there was no answer. Supposedly, the man never left his room. On the floor next to the door was a tray bearing the remnants of a meal. The man had been in the room earlier. Either he had gone out without being seen, or he was inside and was not answering.

Clint decided not to kick the door in himself. He'd let Chief Stewart do that.

He went and found Simon and told him to stand in front of the door until he returned with Chief Stewart.

Clint found Stewart in his office and dragged him back to the hotel, explaining the situation on the way. When they entered the inn Captain Van Allen was in the entry foyer and saw them.

"You can't just break in—" Stewart was saying when they spotted Van Allen.

"What's going on?" Van Allen said. "Clint, have you seen Simon? I need him—"

"He's upstairs, standing guard in front of Bradshaw's room."

"What? Why?"

"Because I told him to."

"But why?"

"I knocked on Bradshaw's door and there was no answer," Clint explained.

"So?"

"So you told me he never leaves the room."

"Maybe he's asleep," Van Allen said, "or just not answering."

"Clint wants me to kick down the door," Chief Stewart said.

"You're the law."

"I can't just kick it down on a whim," Stewart argued.

"He's right," Van Allen said, "he's not going to damage my door."

Frustrated, Clint said to Van Allen, "Then you open it with your key."

Van Allen looked shocked.

"I can't do that," he said. "I've never gone into a guest's room unless I thought something was wrong."

"Okay," Clint said, "I heard someone in the room."

"Someone?" Van Allen asked.

"Doing what?" Stewart asked, catching on before Van Allen did.

"Moaning."

"So you have reason to believe someone in that room might be hurt?"

"That's right."

"What are you two—oh," Van Allen said, finally understanding.

"Henry," Stewart said, "I think I'll have to ask you for your key, or else I'll have to kick the door in."

"Well, all right," Van Allen said, "if you're going to pull rank on me, Chief."

"I'm afraid I'll have to."

Van Allen went into his office and came out with a set of keys.

"Let's go," he said, and led the way up the stairs. Clint and the chief followed.

When they got to the upstairs hall they proceeded to Bradshaw's door. Van Allen told Simon to go back to work.

"Knock once before we go in," Stewart said. "Just in case he is asleep."

Van Allen didn't knock, he pounded, and he called out Bradshaw's name. He made such a commotion that both Mary and Julia Morgan came out of their rooms. Gerald McCrain was still downstairs in the sitting room.

"What is going on?" Julia demanded.

"Is something wrong with Mr. Bradshaw?" Mary asked.

"That's what we're trying to find out, ladies," Chief Stewart said officiously.

"Clint heard someone moaning inside," Van Allen said.

"What?" Julia asked.

"You know," Mary Morgan said, catching on very quickly, "I think I heard some moaning myself."

"You did no such thing," Julia scolded her daughter. "Are you gentlemen going to go into that man's room?"

"That's the plan, ma'am," Chief Stewart said. "Captain Van Allen has a passkey."

"You can't violate that man's privacy," she said.

"We can if there's something wrong," Stewart said. "The man could be injured."

"I heard something," Clint said.

"So did I," Mary said, her eyes shining.

"Poppycock!" Julia Morgan said, frowning.

"We're wasting time, Henry," Chief Stewart said. "While we're arguing out here a man could be dying inside this room. As chief of police, I'm instructing you to open this door."

"I'm opening it, Chief," Van Allen said, inserting the passkey, "I'm opening it."

TWENTY-TWO

Van Allen opened the door and allowed Chief Stewart to enter first, then Clint, and then himself. As he entered he looked back at Julia and Mary Morgan and said, "You ladies better go back to your rooms."

"That's not fair," Mary Morgan said, but Van Allen closed the door firmly behind him.

"Come, Mary," Julia said, dragging her daughter back to their room, "we won't be a party to violating that man's privacy."

"I don't like this," Van Allen said, inside the room.

There was only one room and it was obvious that no one was in it.

"Nothing's wrong," Van Allen said. "He's not asleep, he's not injured, and he's not dead."

"And he's not here," Clint pointed out. "Did you see him leave?"

"No," Van Allen said, "but that doesn't mean he didn't."

Clint walked to the window and found it slightly ajar.

"Here's how he went out," Clint said.

Both Van Allen and Stewart joined him at the window.

"How do you know?"

Clint pointed.

"Scuff marks on the sill," he said. "He's gone in and out this way more than once."

"How does he get down?" Stewart asked.

"He drops down," Clint said. "We're on the second floor, but the ground is higher in the back than in the front. It's not such a bad drop."

"And how does he get back in?" Van Allen asked.

"Well," Clint said, "he leaves the window ajar so he must climb back up."

"Can he do that?" Stewart asked.

"I guess we'll have to go out back and take a look," Clint said.

"Good," Van Allen said, "let's get out of here."

They left the room, locked it, went back downstairs and outside. They walked around the building and stopped beneath the window in question.

"Okay, here," Clint said, pointing to the side of the building. "See the boots marks?"

"There are some handholds here," Stewart said, "but he'd have to be part spider to scale this wall."

"That's weird," Van Allen said. He looked at Clint and Stewart with concern. "Do you think he's the killer?"

"It's possible," Stewart said, "but we can't place him on the island the past four years."

"Unless he's been here under a different name each time," Clint said.

"How do we find that out?" Stewart asked.

"I have an idea about that."

"What is it?"

"Wait."

Clint started to study the ground, moved around until he found what he wanted.

"Lots of tracks back here," he said, "all left by the same pair of boots."

"Bradshaw's," Stewart said.

"Seems obvious."

Van Allen and Stewart exchanged a glance, then looked back at Clint.

"Where do they lead?"

"Well, they mingle, which means he goes the same way every time."

"Can we follow them?"

"Sure."

"Then let's do it," the chief said, "right now."

"Not me," Van Allen said, "this is where I draw the line."

"We don't need you, Henry," Stewart said. "Go on back inside. Clint and I will take it from here."

"You'll let me know what happens when you get back?" Van Allen asked.

"You'll be the first to know, Henry," Clint promised.

"You fellas be careful now."

"We will, Henry," Stewart said, "we will."

Van Allen returned to the house.

"Are you armed, Chief?" Clint asked. He was wearing his holstered double-action Colt today.

"I am," the chief said and showed Clint the cut-down Colt in his shoulder holster. "Do you think this is it, Clint?"

"I don't know, Chief," Clint said, "but we'd better be ready, just in case, don't you think?"

"Oh," Chief Stewart said, "I think."

"Then let's go," Clint said. "I'll take the lead."

"You're the one reading the ground," Chief Stewart pointed out.

TWENTY-THREE

Behind Captain Henry Van Allen's inn there were woods, and Bradshaw's tracks—if that was indeed his name—led right through them.

"He must know his way around these woods," Stewart said, panting as he tried to keep up with Clint.

"From the looks of these tracks," Clint said, "he's been going this way quite a bit."

"Why does he have to sneak out?" the chief wondered. "Who would stop him if he wanted to walk out the front door?"

"Obviously," Clint said, "he made a big deal out of not leaving his room, and not eating with the rest of the guests, setting everyone up to leave him alone, so that when he was gone from his room no one would knock on his door."

"Until you did today."

"Right."

"He's got to be the killer," Stewart said. "Why else would he want to sneak out this way?"

"Could be he's just a thief. Look, the tracks are turning. We're heading toward town now. Are there woods behind the buildings in town?"

"Yes," Stewart said, "many of the stores back up against the woods."

"Have you had reports of anyone breaking into stores in the evenings?"

"As a matter of fact, I have," Stewart said, "but I put those break-ins behind the murders."

"So he's either a murderer," Clint said, "or a thief."

"My guess is murderer."

"Why?"

"Because he sneaked out of the inn now," Stewart said, "and it's only afternoon. The stores and restaurants are still open."

"That's a good point. I see some buildings. We must be parallel to the main street."

Abruptly, Clint stopped.

"What is it?" Stewart asked.

"The tracks split up here. There are several older sets, and then a new set."

"Where do the older sets go?"

"Well, they each seem to head for town, but in different directions."

"I say we should follow the newest set of tracks."

"I agree. Let's go."

They started off again.

"Chief, did you check with the sanitarium and find out if we can get inside?"

"I did," Stewart said. "We can go in and talk to the doctor who's in charge—but why will we have to do that? We've got our man."

"What if we go behind the sanitarium and find these same kinds of tracks?" Clint asked. "Maybe they've got patients slipping out all the time."

"And maybe we'll catch him in the act now."

"I doubt it."

"Why?"

"Because these tracks we're following are a couple of hours old."

They followed the tracks until they suddenly turned and veered toward town.

"Now what?" Stewart asked as Clint stopped.

"They head toward that building."

"That building?" Stewart asked.

"That's it."

"It can't be."

"Why not?"

Stewart folded his arms across his chest.

"That's my building," the man said, flustered. "That's the police station."

"Well," Clint said, "I guess we'd better go and see if he's stolen anything from your desk."

TWENTY-FOUR

"This is odd," Clint said once they were inside the police station.

"What is?" Stewart asked, going through his desk.

"Well, we didn't catch up to him, and he didn't pass us. Apparently, he didn't come in here."

"So?"

"So where is he? He must be somewhere in town."

"Looking for another victim," Stewart said. He stood straight up and looked around. "Doesn't look like anything is missing."

"Are you sure?"

"Well . . ."

"Check your weapons, Chief," Clint said.

"Oh, hell," Stewart said.

He went to a pair of shutters on the wall and opened them. It was a weapons closet, and from what Clint could see there were several Winchesters and shotguns inside.

"Any missing?"

"No," the chief said. "You'd need a key to get these out."

"Any handguns around?"

"No," Stewart said, closing and locking the closet. "Each of my men has his own handgun."

"Is it unusual for no one to be here?" Clint asked.

"Normally, yes," Stewart said, "but with the murder of

the woman I'm trying to keep my men on the street."

"Have you thought about hiring more men?"

"Sure I have, but there's no money in the budget for it, according to our town treasurer."

"Then we'd better get on the streets ourselves," Clint said.

"Maybe one of us better go back to the inn and see if he returned there."

"Good idea," Clint said. "I'll do that. Why don't you meet me there in half an hour. Maybe we can check out the sanitarium."

"Why not," Stewart said. "It doesn't look like I'll be making an arrest today, unless I catch him in the act."

The two men left the police station and split up. Clint walked back to the inn and found Captain Van Allen sitting on the porch.

"What happened?" he asked, rising from his chair. "Did you find him?"

"No," Clint said. "I guess he didn't come back?"

"He didn't come past me."

"Maybe he went back in the window," Clint said. "I'll go upstairs and check."

"I'll wait here."

As Clint entered the inn McCrain approached him, carrying his newspaper.

"What the hell is happening?" he demanded.

"Nothing to concern you, Mr. McCrain."

"Like hell!" the man said. "I'm a guest here and I'm entitled to know if something is wrong."

"Fine," Clint said. "If something is wrong I'll let you know."

Clint left the man standing there and went upstairs. He knocked on the door of Bradshaw's room, and there was no answer. He was in the same predicament as earlier in the day. Either the man wasn't inside, or he was and wasn't answering the door.

"Damn," he said and went back downstairs to the porch.

McCrain was not in the hall to intercept him.

"Well?" Van Allen asked.

"No answer."

"I'm not opening it again."

"I'm not asking you to, Henry. I'm going to walk around back and see if I can see his window. If it's still ajar, then he's not back."

"I'll wait here," Van Allen said again.

Clint went around back and tried to see the window, but it was no use. He thought about climbing the wall, but he didn't have the right shoes, or the talent for it. Shaking his head, he went back to the front.

"No luck?" Van Allen asked.

"The window was only ajar an inch or two," Clint said. "I can't see if it still is."

"What now?"

"Well," Clint said, "we're not going to catch him in the act, that seems certain."

"Where's the chief?"

"Looking around town, in case Bradshaw is there. He's going to meet me here shortly. Say, where's Mrs. McCrain?"

Van Allen shrugged and said, "I haven't seen her."

"And Mary and her mother?"

"Still in their room, I suppose."

"And I saw McCrain down here."

"The scientist is still out there somewhere," Van Allen said. "Are you thinking what I'm thinking?"

"Which is?"

"You know."

"Jessica McCrain and Bradshaw?"

Van Allen nodded.

"Would a man who doesn't like being around people be with Jesse McCrain?"

"I don't know."

"And where would they be? Not in the room she shares with her husband."

"Why not?" Van Allen asked. "Wouldn't that be more exciting?"

"Not for me."

"Then maybe they're at another hotel or inn," Van Allen said. "Or better still, they're out in the woods somewhere, doing it."

"Maybe . . ."

"Are you gonna look for her now?"

"No," Clint said, "let her husband worry about her."

"What if she did go off with him," Van Allen asked suddenly, "and he's killed her?"

"I guess we'll find out about that soon enough," Clint said.

With that he sat down in one of the porch chairs.

"Is that all you're going to do now?" Van Allen asked. "Sit there?"

"What would you have me do?"

"Well," Van Allen said, "you did offer to help find a killer."

"And that's what I intend to do."

"By sitting there?"

"Until Chief Stewart shows up," Clint said, "that's exactly what I intend to do."

Van Allen stared at Clint for a few moments, then shrugged and sat down next to him.

TWENTY-FIVE

By the time Chief Stewart arrived, Bradshaw still had not put in an appearance. It was more than likely that he was back in his room, and the chief was all for kicking his door down.

"You ain't kicking any of my doors in," Van Allen said, shaking his head.

"Then you open it."

"Not again," he said. "You've got no proof that he's done anything."

"Let it go, Chief," Clint said.

"Why should I?"

"Well, for one thing we should go and check the sanitarium," Clint said, "and for another, just plan on being here when Mrs. Livingstone takes Bradshaw's breakfast up to his room in the morning. When he sticks his head out to get it, you can question him."

"That is an excellent idea," Stewart said. He looked at Van Allen. "What time does she take him his breakfast?"

"I'll ask her," he said. "I'll have an answer by the time you come back from across the street."

"All right," Stewart said, looking at Clint, "let's go, then."

"I hope somebody over there confesses," Van Allen said as they walked away.

"You know what?" Chief Stewart tossed over his shoulder. "So do I."

Clint and Chief Stewart were admitted to the sanitarium and shown to the office of the doctor who was in charge. Clint was pleasantly surprised to find out that she was female, and attractive.

"I am Doctor Vivian Longfellow," she introduced herself.

"You're in charge here?" the chief asked, surprised.

"I am for the time being," she said. "The doctor who is actually in charge is Doctor Malone, but he is not on the island at the moment."

"Where is he?" Stewart asked.

"Actually, he's on vacation."

"He leaves this island to go on vacation?" Clint asked.

She looked at Clint and held his eyes with hers, which were gray. Her hair was very black, with some streaks of gray, and it was pulled back into a bun. She was tall, full-breasted, but otherwise slender. She was wearing a white linen coat and had her hands in the pockets.

"For those of us who work here," she said with a smile, "vacation is elsewhere."

"I see what you mean," Clint said.

"So how can I help you gentlemen? Won't you sit down?"

They did, and she sat behind the large mahogany desk.

"This is Doctor Malone's office, isn't it?" Clint asked.

"And what makes you say that? Don't you think a woman could have an office this big?"

"This big, yes," Clint said, "but not this masculine. You are much too feminine for this."

"Why . . . thank you . . . I think."

Clint smiled.

"It *was* meant as a compliment."

"Doctor," Chief Stewart said, trying to get the conversation back to where he wanted it, "we're here to find out if you are missing any patients."

"Why? Have you found one?"

"No."

"Then why do you ask?"

"Surely you've heard about the women who have been killed?"

Dr. Longfellow's lovely face went rigid.

"You're not suggesting that one of our patients is the killer, are you?"

"Doctor, the chief isn't suggesting anything," Clint said. "He's just asking a question."

"We are not missing any patients that I know of," she said coldly.

"Could you check on that?" Stewart asked.

"If there were any patients missing, Chief," Dr. Longfellow said, "I would know about it already. Now if that's all—"

"But it's not," Stewart said.

"What else is there?"

"Have any of your patients ever gotten out—"

"Chief," she said, cutting him off, "this is a hospital, it is not a prison. There are no bars on the windows. Our patients are free to come and go as they please."

"I thought this was a sanitarium."

"It is also a hospital."

"So if a patient wanted to leave the grounds—"

"He or she would be free to do so," she said, finishing for him. "We are not holding anyone prisoner here."

Chief Stewart frowned.

"Doctor," Clint said, "you have a bed check at night?"

Grudgingly, she said, "Yes, we do."

"And has anyone ever been missing at bed check?"

She didn't seem to want to answer that question, but finally she said, "Well . . . perhaps there was . . . once . . ."

TWENTY-SIX

"Would you like to tell us about it?" Clint asked.

"I don't think she has a choice, Clint," Stewart said. "She has to tell us about it."

Clint thought that Chief Stewart, after his visit to the Grand Hotel, was now getting aggressive at the wrong times.

"Why don't you take your time, Doctor," Clint suggested.

"There really isn't much to tell, gentlemen," she said. Her demeanor—once as aggressive as Stewart's—had suddenly changed. "We did have a patient who, for some time, was kept . . . sedated."

"Why?" Stewart asked.

"He displayed some . . . violent tendencies."

"Toward who?" the chief asked.

Dr. Longfellow frowned.

"I don't understand—"

"I think you do, Doctor," Stewart said. "I want to know who he showed violent tendencies to—men, women, people in general?"

"Oh, I see . . ."

Stewart waited a few moments, then said, "Well?"

Clint wanted to know the answer to that question, as well.

"Well . . . he was violent toward some of our nurses."

''Women,'' Stewart said.

''Yes.''

''And what about you, Doctor?'' Clint asked.

''What about me?''

''Was he violent toward you?''

Suddenly, she touched a small scar over her right eye, one that Clint had not noticed at first. It was just above her eyebrow, and maybe a little into it, and she traced it with the little finger of her right hand before she realized what she was doing and stopped.

''Yes,'' she said, ''he was violent toward me.''

''And did he ever . . . leave the grounds?'' Clint asked. He decided not to use the word ''escape.'' ''On his own?''

''Yes, he did.''

''And?''

''And we had to bring him back.''

Clint had the feeling there was more.

''Did he have to be restrained, Doctor?'' Clint clarified.

''Restrained?'' She seemed worried.

''Tied down?''

''Oh . . . well, yes, for a while, but—''

''Is that man still a patient here, Doctor?'' Stewart asked.

''Yes.'' Dr. Longfellow seemed defeated.

''We'd like to see him.''

''I don't think I can—''

''I'm the law on this island, Doctor,'' Chief Stewart said. ''I think you can.''

Helplessly, she looked to Clint.

''I think you'd better, Doctor.''

She tapped the desktop with a fingernail and said, ''All right, but you must be very . . . discreet.''

''We will be,'' Stewart said.

''And quiet.''

''Is everyone asleep?'' Clint asked.

''No, but some of our patients don't react well to . . .

noise.''

Clint was starting to wonder what kind of patients they really had here.

''We'll be as quiet as we can be, Doctor,'' Clint promised.

''Very well,'' she said, standing up. ''Follow me, please.''

Both men stood and followed her to the door, but not before exchanging a look behind her back that said maybe they'd found what they were looking for.

Maybe.

TWENTY-SEVEN

Dr. Longfellow led them down a long hallway with doors on either side. The doors were closed, and had small windows in them, but neither man had the time to stop and look inside.

Following the good doctor was not a hardship, and both men followed the sway of her hips with interest. They exchanged another glance, and this one had nothing to do with patients.

"This is the room," she said, when they reached the end of the hall.

"You keep him on the first floor?" Clint asked.

"Why not?"

"Since he has a habit of . . . wandering, wouldn't it be better to keep him on the second?"

"Who said he had a habit of wandering?" she asked.

"Doctor," Clint said, "let's not play word games. You said he wandered off—"

"He broke his leg," she said impulsively, "one time when he . . . jumped from a window. We keep him on the first floor for his own protection."

"What about the protection of others?" Chief Stewart asked.

Dr. Longfellow tried to save face by saying, "He's only a danger to himself, not to other people."

"How do you know that, Doctor?" Stewart asked.

"How do you know he doesn't go out at night and kill young women?"

"That's ridiculous!"

"Is it?" Stewart asked. "Open the door for us, Doctor. Let's see this man who's a danger only to himself."

There was an orderly in white standing in front of the door. It did not escape Clint's attention that this was the only door with a "guard" on it—and, indeed, this man was large enough to be a guard.

"Open it," the doctor said. The orderly/guard produced a set of keys from his pocket, inserted one into the door lock, and opened it.

"This way, gentlemen," Dr. Longfellow said and started ahead of them. Clint noticed that she was moving unsteadily, and sweating, as if nervous.

"Excuse me, Doctor, before we go in," Clint said.

"Yes?"

"Do you think it's a good idea for you to go in there? I mean, with him tending to be violent toward women."

"That's in the past," she said unconvincingly. "I'm sure I have nothing to fear from Mr. Morgan."

"Is that his name? Morgan?"

"Yes."

"And his first name?"

"Milo."

Clint looked at Stewart, who shrugged. The name meant nothing to him.

"All right, Doctor," Stewart said, "we might as well go in."

TWENTY-EIGHT

Dr. Longfellow opened the door and entered, with Clint and Stewart behind her. The big guard entered last, and stood to one side, hands clasped in front of him.

The man on the bed did not notice their arrival. He was lying on his back, arms at his sides, secured by leather straps. He was a big man, easily larger than the guard by the door.

"This is Milo Morgan," Dr. Longfellow said, standing to one side.

Clint noticed that she didn't get too close to the bed.

Stewart approached the bed and stared down at the unconscious man.

"What's wrong with him? Is he asleep?"

"He's sedated."

"Well, this is no good," Stewart said to Clint. "We can't question him."

"When will he be awake, Doctor?" Clint asked.

"That's hard to say."

"Why?" Stewart wanted to know.

"For some reason," she said, "he reacts to each sedative differently."

"Do you give him the same amount each time?" Clint asked.

"Yes."

"And he doesn't always wake up the same time?"

"That's correct."

"That doesn't sound right."

"Nevertheless, that's the way it is."

"We're wasting our time here," Stewart said, and stormed out of the room.

Clint moved closer to the bed and stared down at Milo Morgan.

"Mr. Adams?" Dr. Longfellow said.

"A minute, Doctor."

He continued to stare down at the man until he saw what he wanted, then turned and wordlessly walked out. The doctor followed and instructed the orderly to lock the door.

In the hall Clint turned and asked, "Why do you lock the door, Doctor, if he's sedated?"

"As I said, Mr. Adams," she replied, "we cannot predict when he will awake from the sedative."

"But he's strapped down."

She hesitated a moment and then said, "Better to be safe than sorry."

Clint smiled and said, "Very professional," and walked down the hall to catch up to Chief Stewart.

Clint and the chief were waiting for Dr. Longfellow in her office when she arrived.

"Oh," she said. "I thought you'd left."

"We need one more thing from you, Doctor," Stewart said.

"And what would that be?"

"A look at Milo Morgan's medical records."

"That's impossible."

"Doctor—" Chief Stewart started, but she cut him off before he could get any further.

"You can tell me all you want that you're the law, Chief," she said, "but unless you have an order from a judge I can't let you see medical records."

"Then answer a question," Clint said.

"What question is that?"

"How long has Milo been a patient here?"

"I'd . . . have to look that up."

"You don't know?" Clint asked.

"He was here when I arrived," she said.

"And when was that, Doctor?" Clint asked.

"Five years ago," she said. "Now, about those records . . ."

"Never mind, Doctor," Clint said, "it won't be necessary. Thank you for your time."

TWENTY-NINE

When they got outside Stewart stopped and turned to Clint.

"That was a waste of time," he said.

"Maybe not."

"How can you say that?"

"Well, for one thing we found out that Milo Morgan has been here for at least five years."

"But we didn't get to question him," Stewart complained. "They keep him sedated. How can he be a suspect if he's sedated all the time?"

"Did you take a good look at him, Chief?"

"I looked at him."

"Did you take a real good look?"

"I guess not."

"Well, I did," Clint said. "If that man was sedated, then so am I."

"What are you saying?"

"That they can't predict when he'll wake up because those sedatives aren't working."

"You're saying he's faking?"

Clint nodded. "And that's why he can wake up whenever he wants."

"What makes you say that?"

"Because," Clint said, "I was staring at him and he felt it. He twitched."

"Don't sedated people twitch?"

"Maybe," Clint said, "but I saw enough to convince me that man was awake and could hear everything we said."

"Well, I'll be—" Stewart turned around and started back inside.

"Don't do that," Clint said. "It won't do any good."

"Then what will?"

"How many men do you have?"

"Four."

"Put two of them on this sanitarium."

"But why would he pretend to be sedated?"

"Maybe so they wouldn't hesitate to put him on the first floor."

"What about the restraints? Wouldn't those hold him?" Stewart asked.

"Did you see the sheer size of him?" Clint asked. "Standing I'll bet he's six eight."

"You think he can break the restraints?"

"He could," Clint said, "but clearly he hasn't yet, or they wouldn't still be using them, they'd be using something stronger."

"Like what?"

"For a man that size?" Clint said. "I'd use chains."

Dr. Longfellow watched Clint Adams and Chief Stewart have their discussion in front of the sanitarium. Stewart made a move as if to come back in, and Clint Adams stopped him. Eventually, they continued walking until they left the sanitarium grounds.

Vivian Longfellow turned away from the window and sat in Dr. Malone's chair behind Dr. Malone's desk. Without realizing it she again touched the scar above her eye, which she had received from Milo Morgan last year. Morgan had grabbed her, put his hands on her, and then tossed her aside, laughing. She had slammed into the wall, opening the cut above her eye. It had taken seven orderlies to subdue Morgan to the degree where he could be sedated. Since then she was always very careful in his presence, being careful to stay out of his reach. She hoped that Clint Adams and the chief had not noticed how frightened she was when they went into Milo's room.

She wondered if the two men could be right. Could it be Milo who was killing those women—had been killing them for the past five years?

Dr. Malone would be back tomorrow. Why couldn't the two men have waited until then to come and ask their questions?

How was she going to explain this to Dr. Malone?

THIRTY

"I understand you used to be a policeman in Pittsburgh," Clint said as they approached Van Allen's inn.

Stewart reacted sharply.

"Who told you that?"

"One of Henry's guests."

"What's his name?"

"McCrain, Gerald McCrain."

"I know the name," Stewart said. "What else did he tell you?"

"Why don't you just tell me what you want me to know?" Clint suggested.

They reached the inn and mounted the porch.

"I had some problems back then," Stewart said. "I drank too much. I have it under control now."

"Fine."

"I do."

"I believe you," Clint said. "We had a beer together the other day, remember?"

"That's right. What did McCrain tell you?"

"The same thing you did," Clint said. "That you had a drinking problem."

"And I got fired."

"Right."

"So why are you interested in my career as a Pittsburgh policeman?"

"Because," Clint said, "I thought you might have some contacts there."

"I do," Stewart said, "one or two."

"Why don't you get a telegram off to one of them and see what you can find out about Milo Morgan?"

"What makes you think he's from the East?" Stewart asked.

"Just a hunch," Clint said. "I think if he was from the West he'd have been hung by now, but just to make sure I'll send a telegram as well. I have a friend in Texas with big ears."

"Okay," Stewart said. "I'll send mine today. I'll get my men into the sanitarium, too."

"Good. Oh, where's the telegraph office?"

"On the same block as my office."

"I'll stop over there later today."

"Stop in my office when you do," Stewart said. "Maybe I'll have something by then."

"All right," Clint said. "See you later, then."

Stewart nodded, quit the porch, and started back toward town. Clint remained on the porch, watching him until he was out of sight, then he sat down and stared across at the sanitarium.

Morgan.

The name struck him all of a sudden. Milo Morgan had the same last name as Mary and Julia. A coincidence? Morgan was, after all, not an uncommon name, but Clint was a firm nonbeliever in coincidence. Perhaps Milo was a relative . . .

His thoughts were interrupted when Henry Van Allen came out.

"There you are. My curiosity is killing me. How'd it go at the sanitarium?"

"Henry," Clint said, instead of answering, "what do Mary and Julia Morgan see when they look out their window?"

"What do they see? Well, I guess they see the sanitarium, and the water beyond it. Why?"

"Did they request a room on that side of the inn?"

"Well, yes."

"Why?"

"I assumed they wanted to see the water. What's this about? Don't tell me you suspect those two women of something now?"

"Henry," Clint said, "with what I've gotten myself into now, I've got to suspect everyone."

"Even me?"

Clint looked up at the old river captain and then said, "Well, maybe not you, Henry—but you might be the only one."

THIRTY-ONE

Clint went upstairs and knocked on the door of the room Mary and her mother were staying in. The door was answered by Julia.

"Mr. Adams," she said, "to what do I owe this pleasure?"

"I'd like to talk to either you or your daughter, Mrs. Morgan."

"Well," Julia said, "since Mary isn't here I guess you'll have to settle for me. Come in."

As he moved past her he caught two distinct scents: a heady perfume and whiskey.

"Where is Mary?" he asked as she closed the door. "She hasn't gone walking alone, has she?"

"I couldn't very well sit on her," Julia said. She walked to the bed and sat down. On the table next to the bed was a metal flask. She picked it up and held it out to Clint. "Would you like a drink?"

"Sure," Clint said, "I could use one."

"You'll have to share the flask with me," she said. "Sorry, but no glasses."

"That's all right."

He took the flask and took a pull from it. The whiskey burned its way down his throat and seemed to spread out in his stomach.

"It's not very good," she said, "but it does the trick."

"Mrs. Morgan," he asked, "are you drunk?"

"Would I let a man in my room if I wasn't?" she asked.

Her usually well-kept hair was tousled. She still had it up, but strands of it had come loose and were hanging down on all sides. Even drunk and slightly disheveled she was a handsome woman. He noticed that she and her daughter shared the same body, except Julia's was a bit thicker here and there, and fuller in the breasts.

"Why are you lookin' at me like that?" she asked.

"I was just thinking how much alike you and your daughter are."

"Alike?"

"Physically."

"Hmph," Julia said, "she has the body I had before I put on weight."

"You haven't put on that much weight."

"Do you find me attractive, Mr. Adams?"

"Very much so, Mrs. Morgan."

She eyed him mischievously.

"Did you come up here with intentions of ravishing me?"

"Why?" he asked. "Are you in need of being ravished?"

"Oh, yes," she said, "very much in need of it."

"Mrs. Morgan—"

"Julia."

"Julia," he said, "if you weren't drunk I would probably take you up on your offer, but—"

"First of all," she said, interrupting him, "it wasn't an offer, it was a question."

She got up and walked around the bed to face him.

"If I was going to make an offer it would be something like this."

She kissed him then, her mouth open, her tongue searching. She tasted of whiskey, but it was far from an unpleasant kiss. In fact, he felt his body responding as she kissed him long and deep, pressing her body against him. The weight of her breasts on his chest was extremely arousing.

"Julia—" he said, but she was having none of it.

"No more talking," she said. "I've wanted to be with you since the first time I saw you."

"Julia, that's the whiskey—"

"Take my word for it, Clint," she said, "I'm not that drunk." She slid her hand between them and rubbed his crotch. "And I don't think this part of you really cares if I am."

She went down to her knees, undid his jeans, and eased his erect penis from his underwear.

"Oh, my," she said, stroking it, first the underside of the shaft, then the top, and then the purpling head. "You are quite a lovely man, did you know that?"

"Julia . . ." he said breathlessly.

She tugged his pants and underwear down to his ankles so she could fondle his balls with one hand while she stroked his cock with the other.

"It's been a long time for me," she said. "A long time. I hope I haven't forgotten how."

She opened her mouth and took just the head of his cock inside. She wet it, licked it, then sucked it, all the while fondling his balls. Then she took more of it into her mouth and for a moment Clint wondered what would happen if Mary walked in at that moment. When the tip of his penis bumped against the back of Julia's throat, however, he forgot Mary, and when her head began to move back and forth, and her lips slid over him again and again, he forgot everything else but her hands, and her mouth . . .

"Julia," he said, gasping, "the bed—"

She allowed him to slide free of her mouth just long enough to say, "After. First I want this."

Her mouth engulfed him again and he didn't resist or try to talk her out of it. She sucked him lovingly, moaning as her lips moved up and down on his slick shaft, sliding her hands around behind him to cup his buttocks, and she took more and more of him into her mouth until finally he couldn't hold back anymore. He exploded into her mouth and almost tripped on the pants and shorts that were around his ankles.

THIRTY-TWO

They moved to the bed after that, as soon as Clint got his boots off, and then his pants and shorts off his ankles. She popped a couple of the buttons off his shirt in her haste to get it off, and he peeled her dress from her, marveling at the fullness and firmness of her body, knowing that with a daughter Mary's age this woman had to be in her late forties, and yet there was no sag to her firm, round breasts. By the time he had her naked, he was erect again. She tugged him onto the bed and urged him into her, saying she couldn't wait.

"It's been too long since I've had a man in me," she said, "and longer still since I've had any satisfaction."

"Your husband—"

"—was like most men," she said, "selfish in bed. You're not going to disappoint me, are you, Clint?"

"Not if I can help it."

He plunged into her, finding her wet and ready. He slid his hands beneath her to cup her firm buttocks and began to move in and out of her. She moaned and clutched him but before long he withdrew, in spite of her complaints.

"What are you doing?" she demanded.

"I'm going to make sure you aren't disappointed."

With that he slid down between her legs and began to work on her with his mouth. He sucked at her, licked her, kissed her, did it all over again while she squirmed and cried out. Finally, his tongue found her rigid little nub and remained there until he felt her belly tremble and she began to buck. He mounted her again then, slid into her and began to take her long and hard. Her nails raked his back, her ankles drummed on his buttocks. Suddenly, with surprising strength she tried to roll him over. He could have resisted, but didn't, and soon she was astride him, laughing and riding him. He reached for her breasts, squeezed them together, and began to lick and bite both her nipples at the same time.

"Oh, God," she said, "oh, Jesus," still bouncing up and down on him, the sound of flesh slapping flesh filling the room, the scent of their excitement mingling with the smell of her perfume, and the whiskey. He watched as her breasts bounced while she rode him, her head thrown back now, a smile fixed on her face, but her breath coming hard and raspy as she sought her satisfaction again.

"Come on," she said to herself—or to him, he wasn't sure—"come on, come on, come . . . on!"

And then her body trembled. He could feel it in her legs and her belly, and as her body was wracked with spasms of pleasure he released himself and erupted inside of her. . . .

"What if your daughter walked in now?" he asked.

She snuggled against him and said, "She'd have to go and get her own man. You know, I thought you were interested in Mary."

"I prefer my women more . . . experienced."

"In fact," she said, "I kind of thought you and she had already—"

"No."

"Somebody marked you," she said, touching the bite mark Jessica McCrain had left on his shoulder.

"Does it matter?"

"Actually," she said, "no, it doesn't. I don't care. You were right."

"About what?"

"You're not selfish the way other men are," she said. "No man has ever been concerned with my pleasure, and no man has ever given me as much as you did today. I won't forget it."

"I won't forget this afternoon, either," he said, "but I think I'd better leave before Mary does come back."

He got up and began to dress. She watched him with pleasure. It had been a long time since she'd watched a man dress . . . afterward.

"That's probably a good idea," she said.

"You know," Clint said, "suddenly you don't seem so drunk."

"You sobered me up," she said. "I guess good sex—great sex—is a sobering experience—at least, for me."

He finished dressing and walked to the bed. He leaned over and kissed her, running his hand over her body as he did.

"You'll get me started again," she said, slapping his hand away.

"Then I'd better leave," he said, and headed for the door.

"Clint?"

"Yes?"

"You came up here for a reason," she said. "What was it?"

He didn't think he should broach the subject of whether or not she had a relative in the sanitarium across the street.

"Like you said, Julia," he answered, "I came up with intentions of ravishing you."

She smiled, reclined onto her back, and said, "And a right fine job you did of it, too, sir."

THIRTY-THREE

Clint shook his head as he went down the stairs to the main floor of the inn. The last thing on his mind when he went to Mary and Julia Morgan's room had been sex—and sex with Julia Morgan even further. Not that she wasn't attractive, but she'd never shown the slightest sign of interest.

As he reached the main floor Mary Morgan walked in the front door.

''Uh, oh, hi, Mary,'' Clint said, as if he had been caught at something.

''Clint. How are you?''

''Oh, I'm fine.'' He knew he was acting guilty, so he went on the attack. ''What were you doing out?''

''I beg your pardon?'' Mary asked. ''Have you suddenly become my father?''

''No, of course not,'' Clint said, even though he'd just slept with her mother. ''It's just that it's dangerous out there. What were you doing?''

''Well, if you must know, I was looking for William Kent.''

''Out by Arch Rock?''

''Yes.''

''That was foolish, Mary.''

''Well, as it turns out he wasn't there, so I wasn't gone very long.''

Long enough, Clint thought.

"Are you all right?" Mary asked him.

"Yes, why?"

"You look . . . I don't know, out of breath."

"I'm fine, really," Clint said. "Look, can I ask you something?"

"What?"

"Something personal."

She hesitated, then said, "You can ask, but I reserve the right to refuse to answer, depending on what the question is."

"All right, that's fair," Clint said. "The chief and I just came back from the sanitarium across the street."

She didn't say anything.

"They have a patient there named Milo," he said, then added, "Milo Morgan," and watched for her reaction.

There was none.

"Mary?"

"What's the question?" she asked. "If there was one, I missed it."

"Do you know a man named Milo Morgan?"

"No."

"He's not a relative?"

"No."

He studied her and came to the conclusion that she was lying, but he decided not to confront her with it, not until he or Stewart found something out from their telegrams—which he still had to send.

"All right," he said.

"That was it?"

"Yes."

"That wasn't so personal," she said. "I thought you were going to ask me something hard."

"No," Clint said, "that was it."

"Then I'll go up to my room, if you don't mind."

"I don't mind," Clint said.

He watched her go up the stairs and hoped that Julia

Morgan had managed to get out of bed and dressed before her daughter came walking in.

When she was gone from sight he went out the door and followed Chief Stewart's directions to the telegraph office. Once there he composed his message and gave it to the key operator to send.

"You gonna wait for an answer?" the man asked.

"You know Captain Henry Van Allen?"

"Sure do."

"I'm at his inn," Clint said. "Bring me the reply there, all right?"

"Whatever you say, mister."

"Tell me something, was the chief in here in the past few hours?"

"Yep, sent a message to Pittsburgh."

Clint wasn't sure why he felt the need to check up on the chief.

"Thanks," he said to the clerk, then left and walked down the block to the police station.

Stewart looked up as Clint walked in, and waved him forward.

"I just came from the telegraph office," Clint said, coming through the small gate and taking a seat.

"Sent mine a while ago," the police chief said. "No answer yet."

"I realized something after you left," Clint said, and told Stewart about the connection he suspected between the Morgan women and Milo Morgan.

"Did you ask?"

"I, uh, asked the daughter, and she said no, but I think she was lying."

"It would make sense that they'd want to stay at Henry's inn, then. They could see the sanitarium building from there. What are you thinking? Son or husband? Son and brother?"

"I don't know," Clint said.

"Maybe you'd better ask the mother," Stewart said. "She might be more inclined to tell the truth."

Clint didn't know what Julia Morgan would be inclined to do next time he saw her. Maybe she'd regret what they had done together. Maybe—like Jessica McCrain—she'd avoid him from now on.

"I've got two of my men on the sanitarium," Stewart said, breaking into Clint's thoughts. "They'll be relieved by the other two tonight."

"That's good."

"Did we ask that woman doctor when the other doctor—what's his name—"

"Malone."

"That's him. Did we ask when he'd be back?"

"I don't think so."

"I'm stupid," Stewart said, scowling.

"You're too hard on yourself," Clint said. "I didn't think to ask, either."

"It's not your job."

"Maybe not," Clint said, "but I could have thought of it, too."

"What do you intend to do with the rest of the day?" Stewart asked.

"Well, I can't afford to miss another of Mrs. Livingstone's meals, so I guess I'll go back to the inn for dinner. Maybe after dinner one of us will get a reply."

"Until then," Stewart said, "I don't know what else there is to do."

Clint stood up.

"Come by tonight after dinner and we'll talk."

"I'll be there."

Clint turned and walked to the door. When he got there he thought of something else to ask, but when he looked at Stewart the man was so deep in thought he decided not to bother him. He'd see him later, anyway.

He left, closing the door gently behind him.

THIRTY-FOUR

Dinner was a quiet affair, with Clint and Henry Van Allen really doing all the talking. Jessica McCrain was still ignoring Clint. He must have really shaken her faith in men. No longer could she be sure that they would always be a disappointment to her.

On the other hand, while quiet, Julia Morgan certainly didn't ignore him. However, neither did she go out of her way to talk to him. He figured Mary must have told her about his questions concerning Milo Morgan. Clint decided to wait until after dinner and then try to corner her to see what she had to say.

As always, Gerald McCrain just kept to himself and ate—and he even did that grumpily.

The two empty chairs continued to stand out starkly, and made Clint wonder once again about the man named Bradshaw. He excused himself, got up, and went into the kitchen.

"Mrs. Livingstone?"

She turned and looked at him, surprised.

"Is there something wrong with the dinner?"

"The dinner is wonderful," Clint said. "When do you bring Mr. Bradshaw his food?"

"Usually after I've finished cleaning up here from dinner. Why?"

"The chief and I want to talk to him, and we feel there's only one way to get ahold of him."

"You want to bring his dinner up?"

"Well, no . . . actually, I hadn't thought of that. Yes, I think I would."

"I'll let you know when I have his tray ready."

"Thank you. I appreciate it, and I'm sure the chief will, too."

Obviously, Mrs. Livingstone was not as protective of Mr. Bradshaw as she was of William Kent. Clint thanked her again and went back to dinner.

"Are you back in the good graces of Mrs. Livingstone?" Van Allen asked.

"Safely nestled," Clint said.

"Good."

After dinner was over Van Allen invited Clint for brandy.

"The chief should be along shortly," he added.

"I'll be there in a minute. I've got to talk with Julia Morgan."

They separated and Clint caught Julia before she went back upstairs.

"Can we talk a moment?"

Julia exchanged a glance with her daughter before agreeing.

"Do you want me to—" Mary started, but Julia cut her off.

"I'm fine, dear," her mother said. "You go ahead upstairs."

Mary gave Clint a look he couldn't quite read and then continued upstairs.

"Let's go in here," Clint said, indicating the living room. The McCrains were nowhere to be seen, and they could be alone there.

"What is it?" she asked. "Do you have any regrets about this afternoon?"

"No, none," he said. "I thought you might."

"I have no regrets about what we did," she said. "I just don't know that we'll ever do it again."

"Mary told you?"

"Yes," Julia said. "Why are you asking such questions of us?"

"Then you do know Milo Morgan."

She took a deep breath and said, "He's my son, and Mary's brother."

"Why should that be so much of a secret?"

"He's had some . . . problems that could be embarrassing to our family."

"Criminal problems?"

"I really don't want to discuss my son with you, Clint."

"Then answer me this, Julia," he said. "Has he ever been violent toward women?"

"You suspect him, don't you?" she asked. "Of killing all those women?"

"He is a suspect, yes."

"Well, it wasn't him."

"Can you be sure?"

She hesitated.

"How long has he been a patient at the sanitarium?" he asked.

"Seven years."

"So he was here all five years that the women were killed."

"Yes."

"But you're sure he didn't do it?"

"Yes, I'm sure."

"Sure the way a mother is sure?"

"You think I'm blind because I'm his mother?" she asked. "I'll have you know that it was me who committed him to that sanitarium. How blind does that make me?"

"Seems to me a loving mother would do that to keep her son out of trouble."

"Have you talked to his doctor?"

"Doctor Longfellow."

"That bi—no, you have to talk to Doctor Malone."

"He wasn't there when we visited."

"He should be back tomorrow."

"How do you know that? You never leave your room."

"Mary goes over there occasionally," Julia said.

"So that's where she goes on her walks."

"Yes."

"Well, at least that makes her safer from the killer—" Clint started, then stopped.

"You think she's in danger from her own brother?"

"I didn't mean that."

"Well, it doesn't matter, really, because he's not the killer. I have to go now."

"Julia," he said as she headed for the hall.

"What?"

"Have you been over there to see him?"

She hesitated, then shook her head and said, "No."

"Why not?"

"He doesn't want me there," she said. "As I told you, I put him there."

"I see."

"I don't think you do, Clint," she said. "I don't think anyone could, except, perhaps, another mother."

She turned into the hall and went up the stairs. That would explain why the closest she got to the place was the view from the window.

But nothing she had said cleared her son of suspicion. She was right about one thing, however. They should go back tomorrow and talk to Dr. Malone.

THIRTY-FIVE

Clint was about to join Van Allen in his study for brandy when the front door opened and Chief Stewart walked in.

"You're just in time for brandy," Clint said, and then remembered the chief's drinking problem. "I mean—"

"I can have a brandy, Clint," Stewart said, cutting him off. "Let's go into Henry's study. I've got something to show you."

They went to the study together, where Van Allen was already imbibing.

"There you two are," he said. "I thought I was going to have to drink alone."

He quickly poured them each a drink and handed it to them.

"I've got something to tell you," Clint said to the chief. "It's about the Morgans."

"I know," Stewart said, "Milo Morgan is their son and brother."

"Who's Milo Morgan?" Van Allen asked.

"The patient we saw in the sanitarium today," Clint said. "How did you find out?" he asked Stewart.

"My contact in Pittsburgh," Stewart said. "He sent me a telegram with everything on it. Milo has a history of violence toward women, and his mother put him in the sanitarium. He was also able to get me the mother and sister's names."

"So that's why they come here?" Van Allen asked. "To see this Milo?"

"The sister sees him," Clint said. "The mother just looks at the place from the window."

"I think we've got our man, Clint," Stewart said. "Now all we have to do is catch him in the act."

"Well, you've got your men in place for that," Clint said, "but tell me, did your contact say anything about him having killed anyone?"

"No," Stewart said, "but I figure the mother put him inside before he could do that."

"And you figure he's been slipping in and out of the place for five years, during the summer, and killing women?"

"Weren't you the one who suggested it first?" Stewart asked.

"I think I suggested we visit the sanitarium, just to be thorough," Clint said.

"So you don't think he's the one?" Van Allen asked. "You still think it's Bradshaw?"

"I don't know that it's either of them," Clint said, "but I think we still need to talk to both of them."

"I'm convinced it's Milo," Stewart said. "My men will watch that place day and night if they have to, until we catch him in the act. If he's going to kill a third woman he's going to have to do it soon."

At that moment there was a knock at the door and Mrs. Livingstone stuck her head in.

"Mr. Adams?"

"Yes?"

"I have that tray ready."

"I'll be right there, Mrs. Livingstone."

She nodded and withdrew.

"What tray?" Van Allen asked.

"I arranged with Mrs. Livingstone to bring Bradshaw's food up to him." He looked at Stewart. "I thought you'd want to tag along."

"I've got my man, Clint," Stewart said. "There's no need to bother with Bradshaw."

"Don't you want to know why he sneaks in and out through the window?"

"It's not illegal," the chief said. He finished his brandy and put the empty glass down. "I appreciate all your help, Clint, but I'm sure it's Milo. Henry, thanks for the brandy."

"Good night, Anson."

The chief left and Clint looked at Van Allen.

"You're not satisfied," the older man said.

"No," Clint said. "I'm going to take that tray up and have a talk with this fella Bradshaw. Do you want to come?"

"I don't think so," Van Allen said. "I'll just stay here and have another drink."

"Fine. I'll let you know what happens."

Clint left the study and went to the kitchen to get the tray.

THIRTY-SIX

Clint carried the tray of food—a plate with chicken and vegetables, the same thing everyone else had for dinner, plus a large glass of water and a pot of coffee—up the stairs, balancing it precariously. He didn't know how waiters and waitresses did this for a living. He had a newfound respect for their ability to balance heavy serving trays.

When he reached the upstairs hall he walked to Bradshaw's door and set the tray down by it. Next, he knocked on the door a few times, then withdrew down the hall to the stairs. Mrs. Livingstone said all she did was leave the tray and knock, and she never knew what happened next.

Well, what happened next surprised Clint. Instead of the door to Bradshaw's room opening, another door opened and William Kent stepped out. The man looked both ways and didn't see Clint on the stairs. He then went down the hall, picked up the tray of food, and carried it back to his room with him. When Kent closed his door, Clint stepped into the hallway and wondered what the hell was going on. There was only one person who could tell him that.

He walked to Kent's room and knocked on the door.

"Just a minute."

It was about a minute before Kent opened the door. He smiled when he saw Clint.

"Mr. Adams, what a surprise. What can I do for you?"

"I need to ask you a few questions, Mr. Kent," Clint

said, and then asked, "or should I call you Mr. Bradshaw?"

"What are you talking about?" Kent asked. "Bradshaw is across the hall."

"Then why did you take his tray of food?"

"What are you—"

"I just saw you come down the hall and take the food, Kent. I should know, I brought the tray up."

Abruptly, Kent stuck his head out the door, looked both ways, then said, "I suppose you had better come in."

Clint entered the room. Kent looked out into the hall one more time, then closed the door and turned to face Clint.

"You've found me out."

"I guess so," Clint said. He looked around and saw the tray on a wooden table. Kent had apparently begun to eat the food.

"Would you like some coffee?" Kent asked.

"You only have one cup."

"I prefer water. I drink some of the coffee just to make Mrs. Livingstone think Bradshaw drank it—so you'd be helping me out."

"Fine," Clint said, "I'll have a cup of coffee, as long as it comes with an explanation."

"It will," Kent said, "I promise."

Kent poured a cup of coffee and invited Clint to sit while he drank it. There was one chair so Clint sat in it while Kent, with his glass of water, sat on the bed.

"I'm not really a scientist."

"No fooling."

"Well, I am, sort of, but what I study is people," Kent said. "You see, I'm here to conduct an experiment about people."

"What kind of experiment?"

"It's about curiosity."

Clint waited and when Kent said nothing else he asked, "What about curiosity?"

"There, you see?" Kent asked. "I didn't continue, and you gave in to your curiosity and asked me to."

"So?"

"I was just making a point."

"Well, keep going, because I haven't got the whole point yet."

"What do you want to know specifically?"

"I want to know about Bradshaw."

"Ah." Kent put down his glass of water so he could use both hands when he spoke. "Bradshaw is an alter ego."

"A what?"

"He doesn't exist, except in the minds of the people who live here."

Clint put the coffee cup down.

"You're not explaining this well enough," he said. "Somebody checked in here as Bradshaw."

"That was me, in disguise," Kent said. "You see, I checked in first as myself, and then as Bradshaw. Then, I made Bradshaw a figure of . . . well, let's say intrigue. He didn't eat with the others, he remained in his room, took his meals there. Do you see?"

"I see what you did, what I don't know is why."

"To make people curious."

"And?"

"To see how they would react."

"Mr. Kent," Clint said, "I don't know how your experiment is going, but I do know one thing."

"What's that?"

"By making Bradshaw a figure of intrigue, you've also made him a murder suspect."

"But that's wonderful!"

"How do you figure that?"

"Don't you see it? The police suspect a man who doesn't exist."

"And you think that's funny?"

"But of course. Can't you see it?"

"All I see is that you might have damaged an investigation and helped a killer stay free by misdirecting the police."

William Kent frowned.

"I didn't think of that. What do you think I should do?"

"You'll have to talk to Chief Stewart and tell him about your experiment."

"But that would give the whole thing away."

"Well . . . you'll still have whatever experiments you've been doing when you leave each morning."

"But I don't have any other experiments."

"What were you doing out by Arch Rock the other day?" Clint asked.

"Same as you, admiring the rock."

"Well, what do you do when you leave each morning? How do you spend your day?"

"Watching this house."

"Why?"

"To see what the people will do."

"And what about leaving the other room by the window?" Clint asked. "What is that all about?"

"I've only done that to further convince people that someone is staying there."

"And you made that trail through the woods?"

Kent nodded happily.

"I just walk back and forth some, flattening the grass down. I do it each day."

"And what about the trail you made to the police station?"

"I haven't gone to the police station."

"You haven't?"

"No."

"Well, somebody has," Clint said.

"I suppose I should go there now, though."

"Actually," Clint said, "there's really no reason to now."

"Why not?"

"The chief believes he's got his man."

"He's made an arrest?"

"No, but he thinks he knows who the killer is."

"And you don't agree?"

"No."

Proudly, Kent said, "You thought it was Bradshaw."

"Yes, I did," Clint said, "so as it turns out, you at least fooled me."

"Then I don't have to give away my experiment to the others?"

Clint thought a moment, then asked, "Did you ever intend to tell them?"

"Well, no. . . ."

"Then don't," Clint said. "For one thing, they may not take it as well as I have."

"You mean they'd be angry?"

"I think so."

"But that's wonderful! They'd be angry at a man who doesn't exist."

"Yes," Clint said, "that would be wonderful."

He left Kent's room, not bothering to tell him that he thought the people in the house would be angry at the man who *did* exist—William Kent!

THIRTY-SEVEN

Dr. Vivian Longfellow approached Milo Morgan's room and told the orderly, "You can take a break, George."

"Thanks, Doctor. I'll be back in half an hour."

"An hour, George," she said. "Make it an hour."

"Sure, Doc."

She waited until the orderly was out of sight and then entered the room. She stood by the door and looked at the man on the bed. She swore she wouldn't do this anymore, but tonight she found herself unable to stop thinking about it.

"Is that you, Vivian?" Milo's voice asked from the dark. He had a deep, resonant voice that sounded as if it were coming from deep within his chest.

"Yes, Milo," she said. "It's me. How did you know?"

"I can smell you, Vivian."

Just hearing him say that excited her even more.

"You couldn't stay away, could you?"

"No, Milo, I couldn't."

"Are you going to untie me this time?" he asked.

"I don't think I can do that, Milo."

"Very well," Milo said, "whatever makes you feel most comfortable. How about a light?"

"Just a little light," she said, "so I can see."

"And so I can see, too."

She turned up the gas lamp on the wall, just a bit, until they could both see.

"Come closer to the bed, Vivian."

She moved closer.

"Undress."

"Yes," she said, and her hands went to the buttons of her white coat. She undid them and removed the coat. She was naked underneath. She had lovely, heavy, rounded breasts with brown nipples, both of which were distended at this point.

On the bed, lying on his back, leather straps holding his arms and legs down, Milo took a deep breath.

"Your scent is even stronger now, Vivian," he said, breathing her in.

She stood by his bed naked and the heavy scent of her readiness, her musk, filled the room.

"Take me out, Vivian."

He was wearing loose-fitting, hospital-issue clothes. He lifted his hips and she tugged down the loose-fitting pants. His penis lay against his belly, large even though it was not erect. She touched it with the middle finger of her right hand, running her fingertip along the underside where the skin was like silk. Unable to help herself she leaned over and ran her tongue over it, wetting it. Slowly, it began to move, to grow, to lift off his belly as it became stiffer, to become erect.

She closed her hand around it now and took him in her mouth.

"Suck it, Vivian," he said breathlessly. "Oh, yes, suck it."

She moaned as she complied, sucking him, riding her head up and down, making him slick with her mouth.

"Mmm, yes, that's it," he said, "stroke it and suck it at the same time."

Vivian Longfellow was an attractive woman, but inexperienced in the ways of sex. Milo Morgan, even though he'd been restrained each time they'd been together, was her teacher, her mentor. Now when she stroked him and sucked him, after months of practice, it was almost expertly.

She joined him on the bed then, leaning over him, and slid his wet penis between her big breasts.

"Mmmm, you've become quite good at this, Vivian," Milo said, "quite good . . ."

His penis slid between her breasts, and the friction was making him throb and grow even larger. Vivian couldn't wait any longer. She mounted him then, sliding him fully into her, riding him, leaning over and dangling her breasts in his face so he could lick and suck them.

"This would be so much more pleasurable for you, Vivian," he said, "if I were able to use my hands."

Her eyes were closed as she continued to ride him up and down. He moved his hips in unison with her, grunting as he came up to meet her downward thrusts.

"Vivian," he whispered, "my hands, undo my hands . . ."

She opened her eyes and he could see how glazed they were. Finally, after months of trying, she was going to do it. He could see that she was going to do it.

"Come on, Vivian," he said, "I want to touch you."

She continued to slide up and down his rigid cock, but she leaned to one side and undid the strap on his right wrist.

"Now the other one, sweetheart," he said, "the other one . . ."

She leaned to her right and undid the strap on his left wrist. When both his hands were free he quickly reached for and grabbed her head in his hands. She seemed startled but had little time to react.

"Stupid bitch!" he hissed, and broke her neck. As her neck snapped he suddenly exploded inside of her. He held onto her, her dead body flopping around as he continued to ejaculate inside of her, and when he was finished he let her go. Her body slid from the bed and struck the ground with a dull thud.

Milo Morgan sat up, rubbed his wrists, and smiled.

THIRTY-EIGHT

Someone was pounding on Clint's door the next morning. He staggered out of bed, unaware of what time it was, and opened it.

"Milo is out," Chief Stewart said.

"Wha—"

"Milo Morgan!" Stewart said. "He escaped last night."

"What? I thought you had two men on the sanitarium?" Clint asked.

"I did," Stewart said. "One in front, one in back."

"And?"

"He killed the one in back."

"Oh, God."

"Will you get dressed? I'll need your help to track him down."

"I don't know the island—" Clint started.

"You know how to track," Stewart said, "and I don't."

"All right," Clint said, "give me a few minutes to get dressed."

"I'll ask Mrs. Livingstone to have coffee and a quick breakfast ready when you come down," Stewart said, "and . . . thanks, Clint."

Clint started to close the door, then opened it and asked, "How did he get away?"

"Doctor Longfellow," Stewart said. "Apparently, she released his hands while they were, uh, having relations."

"And?"

"He broke her neck."

When Clint arrived downstairs it appeared the entire house was awake—except for William Kent and, of course, "Mr. Bradshaw."

"There's something for you to eat in the kitchen," Henry Van Allen said to Clint.

When Clint entered the kitchen Stewart was sitting there. He was eating a piece of bread with marmalade and having a cup of coffee. There were more bread slices on a plate on the table.

"Best I could do on short notice," Mrs. Livingstone said, handing Clint a cup of coffee.

"That's fine, Mrs. Livingstone. Thank you."

Clint slathered marmalade on a piece of warm bread and took a bite.

"Where are your men?" Clint asked.

"They're out looking for Milo Morgan."

"And . . . the dead man?"

"At the undertaker's."

"Was he married?"

"No, thank God."

"Well, before we get started I've got something to tell you."

"What's that?"

Clint told Stewart the story about William Kent and "Mr. Bradshaw."

"Well, that's interesting," Stewart said when he was done, "but it hardly has anything to do with the murders, now does it?"

"No, it doesn't."

They finished their coffee and bread and went back out through the dining room to the front door.

"See here!" Gerald McCrain shouted. Jessica McCrain was clinging to her husband's arm. "We have a right to know why you've disrupted this entire house."

"Have I?" Stewart asked.

"You woke us all banging on his door," McCrain said, indicating Clint.

"I'm sorry if I woke you, Mr. McCrain, but I don't have time to stand here and discuss the matter with you. You see, I've got a killer to catch."

"You know who it is?" McCrain asked.

"Go ahead, Chief," Van Allen said. "I'll explain everything to Mr. McCrain. Good luck to you both."

Stewart looked at Clint and said, "Come on."

"This is where they found Collins, my man," Stewart said.

They were behind the sanitarium and Clint could see where the grass had been pressed down by the man's body.

"He must have lain there a few hours," Clint said. "How did Milo get out?"

He stood up as Stewart pointed to the back of the building.

"That window, two to the right of the door. See it?"

"I see it. Tell me again what he was doing with Doctor Longfellow?"

"She was naked when they found her," Stewart said. "It's not hard to figure out what they were doing."

"Odd," Clint said.

"What's odd?"

"Well, if they'd had sex before, why didn't he kill her then?"

"What do you figure?"

"I think they used to do it with his hands still strapped," Clint said. "I think last night he got her to free his hands, and he finally had a chance to kill her and escape."

"I'll tell you what I find odd," Stewart said. "The other day when she took us into his room she was sweating and nervous."

"Excited," Clint said.

"What?"

"She was sweating, and she was excited."

"You mean . . . sexually?"

"Yes," Clint said, "that can often be mistaken for nerves. I should have seen it."

"Well, let's get to the task at hand," Stewart said. "Can you track him?"

"He's a big man," Clint said, looking at the ground, "and he's leaving a big trail behind him. I can track him."

"Then let's get to it."

"What about your men?" Clint asked. "Don't you want them in on this?"

"No," Stewart said. "I've got them checking the other side of the island. That will keep them out of our way—and his."

"Ah," Clint said, "you're afraid he'll kill another one."

"I'm going to make sure he doesn't kill another woman, or another one of my men."

"Oh," Clint said, "I assume he took your man's gun?"

"No," Stewart said, "he didn't."

"So he's unarmed?"

"He is."

"That ought to make him easier to take."

"I'm not going to take him," Stewart said, "I'm going to kill him."

"That's not very professional, Chief."

"I'm not feeling very professional, Clint," Chief Stewart said. "Not very professional, at all."

THIRTY-NINE

They tracked Milo into the woods, with Stewart right on Clint's tail.

"Did your Pittsburgh contact tell you where Milo was from?"

"I believe the family is from St. Louis," Stewart said. "Neither of the women told you that?"

"No," Clint said, "neither of them was very forthcoming about him."

A couple of hours later Clint said, "He's not lost in the woods."

"What do you mean?"

Clint turned and faced Stewart.

"I mean he knows what he's doing. He's not a tenderfoot. Living in St. Louis he probably learned how to track, and so he knows how not to be tracked. I've followed a couple of false trails already."

"So does this mean you can't find him?"

"It means we need more men," Clint said. "If he's going to lay false trails then we need someone to follow them and determine that they are false."

"My men don't know anything about tracking."

"I can give them a quick course, or . . ."

"Or what?"

"What about the fort?" Clint asked. "Would they give you some soldiers?"

"They probably would," Stewart said. "That's a great idea."

"Let's go back, then."

"But we'll lose him."

"Can he get off the island?"

"Not on the ferry," Stewart said. "I've got that covered."

"Are there any other boats on the island?"

"There could be," Stewart said, "small ones that I don't know about, but not large ones."

"Well, he's been on the island seven years, but for the most part he's been locked up. He probably doesn't know his way around real well. It'll take him some time to get his bearings, and we can use that time, as well. Come on, we'll go back and organize a proper search. If we can get to him before he stumbles across a small boat—"

"Even if he finds a small boat it'll be slow going, especially if he's not experienced," the chief said. "Also, I'll have someone watch the water. If he's trying to get off the island that way we should be able to spot him and catch him with the ferry."

"Sounds like we've got everything going our way," Clint said.

"Except for one thing," Stewart said.

"What's that?"

"He might kill another woman before he's through."

They returned to the inn, and then Stewart took his leave to find his men and go to the fort to ask for soldiers.

As Clint entered the inn Van Allen met him in the front hall.

"This came for you," he said, handing Clint a telegram.

It was from Rick Hartman, in Labyrinth, Texas, and it told Clint most of what he already knew about Milo Morgan, his mother, and his sister.

"What is it?"

"Just confirmation of what we already know," Clint

said, "and one extra thing that Milo Morgan's mother didn't tell us."

"What's that?"

"It appears he was a suspect in the disappearance of two women in St. Louis."

"Were they found?"

"No."

"And he wasn't arrested?"

"There was no evidence."

"And it was only two women?"

"Yes."

"But that doesn't match the pattern here."

"Maybe," Clint said, "his mother put him away before he got to a third woman."

"Maybe."

"And maybe," Clint said, "he's not the killer."

"But Anson said he killed that doctor," Van Allen said. "And he's on the run."

"What if she's the first woman he's ever killed? Wouldn't he still be on the run?"

"I suppose so."

Clint looked up, ostensibly at the second floor.

"Someone should tell his mother and sister what's going on."

"Um . . ."

"You already told them?"

"I thought someone should," Van Allen said, "but maybe you could go and talk to them, anyway. They're probably worried sick."

"If I go up there," Clint said, "they're probably going to lie to me."

"What's the point in lying now?"

"I don't know," Clint said. "I guess I'd better ask them that, too."

FORTY

Clint went upstairs and knocked on the door of the Morgan room. Mary opened the door.

"Oh, it's you," she said. "Have you killed my brother yet?"

"Your brother killed a woman last night," he said. "Doctor Longfellow."

"I don't believe that."

"It's verified," he said. "There's nothing to disbelieve."

"Let him in, Mary," Julia said from inside the room. "He can tell us something."

"Like what?" Mary asked. "How many men are after Milo?"

But she moved out of the way and let Clint enter the room, closing the door after him. She turned, folded her arms across her breasts, and glared at him.

"How many men are after him, Clint?" Julia asked. She was sitting in a chair by the window.

"I don't know, Julia," Clint said. "He killed one of Chief Stewart's men. The other three are looking for him, and the chief has gone to the fort to ask for soldiers to help."

"Help kill him," Mary said.

"He's dangerous, Mary."

"Does he have a weapon?"

''No,'' Clint said, ''but he's broken two people's necks. It appears he doesn't need a weapon.''

''You can't prove to me he killed them,'' she said. ''All you know is that he's on the run. He could just be scared.''

''I've seen your brother,'' Clint said, ''the size of him. He doesn't strike me as the type to be scared.''

''He is, you know,'' Julia said. ''He's always scared, always has been. Inside, he's more little boy than man.''

''Julia,'' Clint said, ''what happened in St. Louis?''

''How did you find out about that?'' Mary demanded.

''I did some checking.''

''And what exactly did you find out?'' Julia asked.

''That two women went missing and are presumed dead,'' Clint said. ''Young women.''

''They couldn't prove anything.''

''Of course not,'' Clint said. ''You whisked him away to the island before they could.''

''He didn't kill those women!'' Mary said.

''Can you prove that?''

''We don't have to,'' she said with a grim smile. ''It's the law's responsibility to prove he did, and they couldn't.''

Clint turned away from Mary and looked at Julia.

''What about it, Julia?'' Clint asked. ''What do you believe? Or are you in denial like your daughter?''

''You don't have to tell him anything, Mother.''

Julia looked at her daughter, and then out the window at the sanitarium.

''I hoped,'' she said, ''I prayed that they could help him in that place.''

''Mother, don't say anything more.''

''Mary,'' Julia said, ''he's killed two people . . . and we don't know about . . . about all those women all these years—''

''I won't listen to you!'' Mary said, cutting her mother off. She turned, stormed out of the room, and slammed the door.

''She loves him very much,'' Julia said.

"So do you."

"Yes," she said, "I do, but maybe I can't help him anymore."

"Julia," Clint said, "do you think he's been killing these women all these years?"

She hesitated a moment, then said, "No . . . but I know he killed the doctor and the policeman last night. I'm not so foolish as to believe differently—and I'm not in denial."

"But not the girls?"

"No." She turned away from the window and looked at him. "Do you?"

"I don't see how he could have gotten out each time," Clint said, "over and over."

"He got out last night."

"Yes," Clint said, "but he had to kill two people to do it."

"Clint," she said, "are you going to help them kill my boy?"

"Julia, I'm going to help track him. I'll try to bring him back alive, but . . ."

"I understand," she said wearily. "If he resists, they'll kill him—and he will resist."

"Tell me something," Clint said. "Do you think he'll try to see you?"

"I doubt it," she said. "He would never see me when I visited."

"What about Mary?"

"He might—" She started, then stopped short. She looked stricken. "Oh, my God. If she tries to find him she could get hurt, Clint. She could get in the way."

"Don't worry," Clint said. "There's no big search party yet. I'll find her and bring her back."

"Oh, God," she said, "I can't lose both of my children, Clint, I can't."

"I'll do my best to bring them both back, Julia," he said. "I promise."

FORTY-ONE

Clint went downstairs and looked for Mary Morgan until he was convinced she wasn't in the house. He found Van Allen sitting in his study.

"How'd it go?"

"Not well," Clint said. "Mary stormed out, and her mother is afraid she might do something stupid. Have you seen her?"

"No," Van Allen said, "but I've been in here since you went upstairs."

"If she went out, there's no telling where she went."

"Would she be trying to find her brother?"

"Maybe," Clint said, "but I can't believe she'd be that silly. She's a smart girl, but how would she know where to look on the island . . ."

"What?" Van Allen asked when Clint stopped.

"She is a smart girl, isn't she?"

"I guess so," Van Allen said, "I don't know her that well—"

"How would she know where to look for him?"

"You just said she wouldn't."

"That's right," Clint said, "unless she arranged it beforehand."

"You mean, when shc visited him? How could she know he'd break out?"

"What if she said to him, just in case you ever break out meet me . . . where?"

"I don't know," Van Allen said, "where?"

"That's the question."

"I know," Van Allen said as Clint headed for the door, "but what's the answer?"

Clint started for the stairs. If anyone would know where Mary would arrange to meet her brother, it would be her mother. However, he stopped at the foot of the stairs as he got an idea. If Mary was going to meet him, she'd want to bring him food.

He changed direction and went to the kitchen.

"You're getting to be a regular in here," Mrs. Livingstone said.

"I'm sorry to bother you, Mrs. Livingstone, but have you seen Mary Morgan in the past few minutes?"

"As a matter of fact, I have," the cook said. "She came in just before you did, asked if I had some cold chicken from last night. As it happens, I did, and I gave it to her."

"That was all?"

"That's all I had. Oh, she took an empty container, said she was going to fill it up with water. Doesn't sound like much of a picnic to me."

"She said she was going on a picnic?"

"Yes."

"With whom?"

"She didn't say, but I assumed it was either you or that nice young Mr. Kent."

Or her brother, Clint thought.

"Thanks, Mrs. Livingstone."

Now it seemed pretty certain she was going to meet her brother, or else why bring food?

The question was, where were they going to meet?

"I don't know," Julia Morgan said when Clint put the question to her. She was still sitting in front of the window.

"Julia, if you're covering for them it's not going to help."

"I'm not," Julia said, but Clint knew she was lying.

He leaned over and looked out her window. Across from them was the sanitarium. If he stood to the left he could see the road to town, but if he stood to the right he could see . . .

"That's it," he said.

Julia was sitting just to the right of the window. He'd thought she was looking at the sanitarium, but she wasn't looking at that at all.

"I know where they're meeting," Clint said. "You've been looking at it all along."

"Clint—"

But he was out the door. You couldn't see the whole thing from her window, but you could just make out the tip of Arch Rock.

FORTY-TWO

It was so simple. Where else could she possibly have told her brother to meet her? The only things on the island more noticeable or easier to find than Arch Rock were the fort and the Grand Hotel. Arch Rock was perfect.

Clint hurried from the inn to the rock, hoping to find Milo and Mary and catch them off guard. He wanted to be able to bring Milo in alive.

As he approached the rock he slowed down. He heard voices, and then as he rounded the bend he saw them, sitting at the base of the rock as if they didn't have a care in the world. Milo, in his hospital clothes and filthy, was taking great bites from the remains of a chicken.

"How can we get you off the island?" Mary was asking him.

"I don't know," Milo said, "but I don't want to go back to that hospital."

"You won't have to, Milo," she said, touching his face. "I'll take care of you."

"You won't tell Mom, will you? She'll send me back."

"No," she said, "I won't tell Mother."

Milo looked out at the water.

"Maybe I could swim."

"You'd never make it," she said. "It's too far."

"Then we need a boat." He looked at her. "You'll have to find me a boat, Sis."

"I'll find one, Milo, I promise." She stroked his face. "My poor Milo. What did they do to you in there all these years?"

She continued to stroke his face, and then she leaned forward and kissed him, only her affection did not seem very sisterly.

Clint decided to step forward and end it.

"Milo!" he called.

Milo looked at him, frowning strangely, but showing no surprise, and no fear. Mary, however, was shocked to see him, and pulled her hand away from Milo's face.

"How long have you been there?" she demanded.

"Long enough."

She closed her hand into a fist, the hand she had been stroking her brother's face with.

"We . . . didn't do anything wrong."

"I'm think I'm beginning to see one of the reasons your mother wanted to put Milo away, Mary."

"It wasn't his fault," she said. "It was mine. I . . . seduced him when we were young."

"I really don't care to hear this, Mary," Clint said. "Milo, I have to take you back."

"Who are you?" Milo asked, then his frown smoothed. "Oh, yes, I saw you in the hospital. You're the one who knew I wasn't asleep."

"That's right."

"Are you a policeman?" He was still holding the chicken in one hand.

"No, Milo, I'm not a policeman. I'm just someone who's trying to help."

"Help me?"

"Help everyone, if I can."

Milo laughed, a deep, rumbling sound.

"That can't be done."

"Maybe it can."

"No," Milo said. "If you want to help the police, then you don't want to help me."

"Just come back with me, Milo," Clint said. "We'll talk about those women."

Milo frowned again.

"The ones in St. Louis?"

"Sure," Clint said, "and the ones here."

"I didn't touch any women here," Milo said, looking confused.

"And the ones back home?"

"He doesn't know anything about them," Mary said.

"Sure I do," Milo said. "I know where they are."

"How do you know, Milo?"

"Because I buried them."

"After you killed them?"

"I didn't kill them," Milo said, "I just hid them."

"Milo," Mary said, "hush."

Clint studied the brother and the sister, and suddenly had a sick thought.

"You did it," he said to Mary. "You killed the women in St. Louis. He buried the bodies to protect you."

She looked at Clint and lifted her chin.

"They were whores," she said. "They were . . . trying to take him away from me."

A sister so jealous of her brother that she killed two women who were interested in him—or were they? Perhaps they were just innocent women whom she saw as a threat. Whatever the reason, she had killed them, and her brother had protected her. Even when his mother had him put away he hadn't told. Suddenly, Clint wondered if Julia knew the whole story, as well.

"I think we should all go and talk to Chief Stewart."

"No police, Clint," Mary said. "Milo, don't let him go."

Milo dropped the chicken and stood up.

"What about Doctor Longfellow, Milo?"

"He told me what she'd been doing to him for months," Mary said. "It was disgusting. I told him to kill her first chance he got."

"And the policeman?"

"He got in my way," Milo said. "I told him not to, but he did."

"And now I'm in your way, Milo?"

"We have to get away, Clint," Mary said, "and we can't let you stop us. Milo!"

Milo started down from the rock, a purposeful look on his face.

Clint drew his gun.

"Mary," Clint said, "if he comes near me I'll shoot him."

"You won't," she said. "He's unarmed."

"He's over six and a half feet tall," Clint said, "and he breaks people's necks. I don't consider that unarmed."

"I know all about your code of the West, Clint," she said. "I've read all the books. You don't shoot unarmed men."

"Stay back, Milo," Clint said, pointing his gun. "Don't listen to her."

"Go ahead, Milo," Mary said. "Don't worry, he won't shoot you."

Milo continued toward Clint.

"Sorry, Milo," Clint said and shot him in the left leg.

Milo's thigh was like a tree trunk. He stopped for a moment, then kept coming. Clint had no choice.

"You've been reading the wrong books, Mary," he said, and shot Milo through the heart.

FORTY-THREE

Clint followed the path that led from the back of the police station into the woods. Once in the woods it branched out into several paths, all of them beaten down as if used often.

It was the morning after he had shot Milo Morgan to death. Mary Morgan was in a cell in the police station. The mayor and the whole town were ecstatic that the killer had been brought to justice. Naturally, Julia Morgan was not speaking to him. She had been hoping not to lose both children, and while Mary was still alive, she most certainly had lost both. Clint didn't bother telling her about Milo and Mary's relationship, but he did tell Chief Stewart that Mary had killed the two women in St. Louis.

Clint had done some heavy thinking during the night and had come to the conclusion that he believed Milo, that the big man had not killed the women who had been slain over the past five years. If that was true—and if Mary hadn't done it—then the killer was still loose. It was then a coincidence—much as he hated the word—that the killer of the St. Louis women had ended up on this island at this time.

That was why he was in the woods, retracing some of the worn footpaths. Indeed, there were paths that were years old, where the grass had not grown back, and yet which had not been heavily traveled for a time. However, the path leading from the back of the police station had been recently used, and Clint realized that there was a suspect who had been on the island each of the past five years who nobody had ever mentioned—least of all Chief Anson Stewart.

Before presenting his theory to the chief, he decided to run it by Captain Henry Van Allen.

"It's impossible!" Van Allen said.

They were in his study with the door closed. The Morgan women were no longer guests, and even the McCrains had checked out that morning. The only guests left were William Kent and "Mr. Bradshaw."

Before leaving, Jessica McCrain had pulled Clint aside.

"I realize I've acted strangely since . . . that night, but I've decided that you did me a favor."

"I did?"

"Yes," she said. "You've shown me that I don't have to settle. When we get home I am going to divorce my husband, take as much money as I can from him, and then find a man who can satisfy me."

"Then I wish you luck."

"You, uh, wouldn't be looking for a wealthy divorcée, would you?"

"I'm afraid not, Jesse," he said. "Good luck."

Now he was in Van Allen's study, ready to defend his theory.

"Not impossible, now," Van Allen said, changing his own mind, "improbable and yet it makes sense . . . but I still can't believe it. Why?"

"I guess I'll ask him," Clint said, "but my guess is he's sick."

"How could he be, and no one noticed?"

"Because he keeps it under control, apparently a year at a time. Somehow, this time of the year—summer—brings it out."

"Tourists," Van Allen said, "there are a lot of them here

in the summer, walking around, sightseeing, some of them alone . . ."

"Which makes them good targets."

"Exactly." Van Allen remained silent for a few moments, deep in thought, before speaking again. "When will you confront him?"

"Today," Clint said, "now."

"What if he doesn't admit it?"

Clint shrugged.

"I can't prove it, Henry. I'll be stuck. It will be up to you."

"What can I do?"

"Talk to the mayor, make your case—"

"*Your* case!"

"Make the case and dump it in the mayor's lap." Clint stood up.

"What if he tries to kill you?"

"I don't think he will," Clint said. "He's used to killing women. A man kills women because he hasn't got the nerve to try to kill a man."

"I hope you're right."

"So do I, Henry," Clint said and left.

FORTY-FOUR

When Clint entered the police station there were three men there. The chief was behind his desk, and two of his men were standing off to one side. Clint knew that the chief would not even talk to him if the men were present.

"Clint," Stewart called out, "come on in."

Clint went through the little swinging gate and leaned on Stewart's desk. He spoke so only the chief could hear him.

"Tell your men to get out."

"What? Why?"

"We have something to talk about," Clint said. "Something you're not going to want them to hear."

"Like what?"

"Like murder."

"What do you—"

"Take my word for it," Clint said, cutting him off. "Send them out on patrol, or something."

Stewart stared at Clint for a moment, then looked over at his men.

"You fellas go out on patrol."

"We just got—" one of them started.

"Out!" Stewart shouted. Apparently, he had no trouble asserting himself with subordinates. Or maybe all that business of being intimidated by people with money was a lie?

"What's on your mind, Clint?"

"I think you know."

Stewart sat back in his chair and assumed an expression Clint had never seen before—arrogant, self-satisfied, in control.

"Enlighten me."

"All right," Clint said, sitting down, trying to show as much calm. "You killed those women."

"Which women?"

"The fourteen women who have been killed on this island over the past five years. You know, I think I just figured out why you never got any federal help out here."

"And why's that?"

"Because it's your job to ask for it, and you never did."

"When did you decide all this?" Stewart asked.

"I thought it over last night. You're the only person who has been on the island for the past five years that nobody suspected."

"So you decided to suspect me?"

"I took a look out behind the police station," Clint said. "There's a path worn into the grass, but it doesn't lead from the woods to the station, it leads from the station to the woods. That's the path you took whenever you wanted to leave here without being seen."

"That's your proof?"

"You'll be happy to know, Chief, that I don't have any proof. None at all. All I've got is what I thought, and what I now know."

"Now you know?" Stewart asked. "You didn't before?"

"I only suspected, up until just a few moments ago, when you showed your real face. You were very good with your act about you and rich people."

Stewart said nothing.

"If I was to check you out myself with the Pittsburgh police, would I find that you were on a case dealing with violence toward women? Young women?"

"I don't know," Stewart said. "Why don't you check?"

"Why don't you just tell me if I'm right?" Clint asked.

"There's just you and me here. You've had everybody fooled for five years, Chief. That's quite a feat, I think."

Clint was hoping the man would admit it, but Stewart just looked at him. What the hell, Clint thought. What's the difference? Look at him. The look on his face was all the proof Clint needed. If he could have gotten away with it, he would have shot Anson Stewart there and then, but how would he explain killing a policeman with no proof?

"Not going to give in, huh?"

"You shot the killer, Clint," Stewart said. "Everybody knows that."

"Yeah," Clint said, "they do know that."

"I think it would be a good idea for you to leave this island," Stewart said, leaning forward. "Don't you?"

"Can't be soon enough for me," Clint said, standing up. "I'll be on the first ferry in the morning."

"I hope you'll forgive me if I don't see you off," Stewart said. "This little incident has sort of soured me on our budding friendship."

"Don't worry," Clint said. "I won't miss you."

Clint stood there a moment, staring at the man.

"You wish you could do it, don't you?" the police chief said. "Draw your gun and shoot me right now."

"It would be nice."

"Like you said," Stewart replied, "you've got no proof."

Clint decided there was nothing left to say. He just turned and walked out.

The next morning Captain Henry Van Allen walked with Clint down to the ferry. They watched as Duke was loaded onto it. Once on the other side Clint would give the big horse the exercise he had so sorely missed since being on the island.

"I don't know what to do or say," Van Allen commented. "I still find it hard to believe."

"I can only tell you what I saw in his face, Henry,"

Clint said. "He became a man I hadn't seen before."

"A man I've never seen."

Clint put his hand on Van Allen's shoulder.

"I hate to leave this in your hands, Henry, but he's your friend. Watch him. There's still time left in the summer, and only two women have been killed."

"But surely, even if you're right about him, he wouldn't kill a third woman, not now that everyone believes the killer is dead."

"Henry," Clint said, "I don't know that he has a choice. If I'm right, then he's killed three women a summer for four years, and two so far this summer. It's a compulsion, and one he might not be able to control."

Clint turned and boarded the ferry, then turned to Van Allen, who stood forlornly on the dock.

"Watch him, Henry," Clint said. "Watch him closely."

Clint stood at the rail of the ferry and watched the island recede behind him. He didn't like leaving Van Allen on the island with a killer, but what else could he have done? Who on the island would believe him?

Maybe that was the key. Maybe that was the proper question. Who *on the island* would believe him? Maybe, if he went somewhere else, spoke to the law somewhere else, they'd believe him. But where? Federal? Certainly not in the west. It had to be someone, some police department close by, or—and then it hit him. Maybe it had to be a police department that was familiar with Stewart.

Like Pittsburgh.

When Clint had threatened to check with the Pittsburgh police about whether or not Stewart had a record of violence the man had told him, "Go ahead." Was that because he wasn't afraid, or because he'd been bluffing?

The only way to find that out was to go to Pittsburgh and ask. Maybe there was not only a record of violence, but a string of unsolved murders of young women.

Clint turned away from the rail, satisfied that he had a

course of action, and found himself looking down the barrell of Chief Stewart's gun.

"You're surprised to see me," Stewart said.

"Actually, yes."

"You didn't think I'd just let you walk away, did you?" the man asked.

"Yes, I did," Clint said. "After all, what could I prove?"

"Yes," Stewart said, "that was what I thought originally. What could you prove, but then I thought, what could you prove here?"

Clint had the uncomfortable feeling that their minds had been on the same track, only Stewart's had gotten there first.

"So I thought, who else could you talk to, and I came up with one answer."

"The Pittsburgh police."

"Exactly."

"So there probably are a few unsolved murders on the books in Pittsburgh, huh? Murders of young women?"

"Probably."

"So go ahead and shoot, then," Clint said. "What are you waiting for? Oh, maybe your shots would alert the captain of this ferry? Or his crew?"

"And what if it did?" Stewart asked. "I'm the Chief of Police, after all. I'd just say I was apprehending a criminal—maybe even the murderer."

"Go ahead, then," Clint said, "or is killing young women more your style? Maybe you can't pull the trigger on a man who's looking at you, huh?

"Oh, I can pull it," Stewart said. "I have to. I don't have a choice."

"Well," Clint said, "neither do I."

He could count the times he'd drawn on a gun that was already out and covering him on one hand, but he was still here, still alive. When he needed it, that little bit of extra speed—even beyond his usual blinding speed—was there.

Of course, having a man holding a gun on you who wasn't fully prepared to use it, who wasn't *used* to using it, was a help.

When Clint drew and fired Chief Stewart's eyes bulged in surprise as the bullet struck him in the chest. Still holding his own gun on Clint he was suddenly unable to pull the trigger. His entire system was shocked and paralyzed and all he was able to move was his mouth as he started to ask, "How—" before he was cut off by a flood of blood from his mouth.

Clint stepped aside as the man fell onto his face.

"It helps," he told the corpse, "if you don't hesitate."